PELICAN MOON

Daniel Hance Page

© 2002 by Daniel Hance Page.
All rights reserved.

No part of this book may be reproduced,
stored in a retrieval system, or
transmitted by any means, electronic,
mechanical, photocopying, recording, or
otherwise, without written permission
from the author.

ISBN: 1-4033-4066-8 (e-book)
ISBN: 1-4033-4067-6 (Paperback)

This book is printed on acid free paper.

1stBooks - rev. 07/30/02

For Dr. Tom M. Pauk, the best doctor who even makes house calls in 2002.

Oct. 12, 2002

"For there is another kingdom beneath the water, deep and blue, where the treasures of the sea are only discovered by a certain few."

Moonstar

For
the people at Belleair Beach, 1997.

ONE

THE SHARK

Sethrum Moon shoved a large hook through a mangled barracuda before dropping this bait into inky water that was always restless even during an evening without wind. The reeking barracuda vanished quickly beneath moonlight dancing on the water's surface. While this bait descended, fish line moved between Sethrum's fingers that were scarred from tooth, hook and knife cuts. He stopped the descent once to wash fish slime from his hands. Drying his hands on his jeans, he thought, there must be sharks here. He resumed releasing the line.

Daniel Hance Page

The lone man in the canoe was tall. His muscles worked with the skill of a person accustomed to being busy. His scars told of mishaps that come to people who are always working or striving at something. His hair was black with gray streaks. His brown eyes could usually detect something interesting in life regardless of harsh circumstances. Depth and tenacity in his character had brought him through to a variety of accomplishments although he rarely spoke of them, causing himself to be underestimated by many people.

The Gulf of Mexico teems with life, noted Sethrum. The water brings a wilderness right up to the shore. I can watch the shoreline endlessly without tiring because there is constant action involving changing tides and creatures along with people who come to watch or fish. For the Gulf, my canoe is a frail craft yet it's good for bringing the bait a long way out from shore. Maybe I came out too far this time; but I would like to catch a shark. The line released smoothly, so my fishing pole must still be in the sand spike next to my truck. With a wrong move in this canoe, I could become shark bait myself. I'm a bit of a worrier, I know. However, my interests take me beyond worry.

With force similar to the power of the water itself, something hit the line, wrenching it across Sethrum's hands. Beads of water jumped from taut line pointing into murky depths. While shooting downward, the line loosened from the shore.

"What have I hit now?" whispered Sethrum, partly in shock as he struggled to keep his hands from getting tangled in the slithering and rapidly descending line. "I can't catch a shark now," he told the dark, undulating water. "I don't want to get anything while I'm in this canoe. I'm just bringing out the bait."

Using the back of his arm, he wiped sweat from his forehead. His throat was dry and his nerves had flared making him feel tense; but he knew he was not going to let go of the line or cut it. Sure, he told himself disparagingly, wouldn't I be just the type to hold on to the line. I'm also the type to use a canoe to bring the line out far enough to catch a shark. Small sharks swim close to shore. Larger fish usually stay out farther. I like trying for the larger quests and something big just caught me. The shark has trapped me in this little canoe. Hooking a fish large enough to catch me is my ultimate fishing dream—or nightmare. Any person who likes to fish probably feels the same way. Such a once-in-a-lifetime chance has happened to me. I'm going to hold on and not let this thing go.

All possible line must have unwound from the reel, noted Sethrum. I can feel the pole being dragged through the water. I will pull my pole to the canoe

Pelican Moon

then wind in the line. If I can get a fishing rod in my hands again, I can fish normally and have a greater chance to catch this powerful thing on the other end of my line. If I work the line carefully, I can tire the shark and guide it to shore. Fishing from a canoe was not my idea. I have something big on now and I'm not going to let it go. I'm supposed to only use the canoe to set the line. I'm sure though that this fish will soon get tired. I'll turn it to the north toward shore. I can clearly see lights on the land. In the other direction, there are lights from a few ships. Beneath me, there is a large shark. I must not get lost out here.

A burst of line shooting downward tugged against the canoe and brought a sheet of water splashing over the side. A quick release of line stabilized the craft while water swirled menacingly along the floor. Working rapidly, Seth used a bailing can to remove most of this water.

The hidden fish ended its powerful rush and commenced a steady, pulling movement, forcing the fragile craft to slice through the Gulf's calmly undulating surface. The sheen of moonlight divided to let the canoe pass. This craft was pulled steadily on a silver ocean.

If the fish goes too far out from shore, thought Sethrum, I'll cut the line. Meanwhile, I will keep a good hold on the shark and continue bringing in line from my fishing pole. After I've pulled the pole to my canoe, I can use the pole to catch this fish. The shark just got lucky and bit before I was ready.

The line swung violently, knocking Seth to the floor of his canoe. Water poured over the side again. Managing to keep a grip on the line, he released some to the shark. Almost frantically, he also worked to drag the rod closer until this welcome piece of equipment came into view. He grabbed the rod and brought it into his canoe.

With a fishing pole in his hands again, he felt like he was more in control of the situation. He quickly reeled in loose line from the floor of the canoe. In a short time, the rod bent toward a silver Gulf where a large shark swam steadily along a course which seemed to be parallel to the distant shore.

If the wind starts blowing, I'll have to cut the line, Sethrum warned himself. There are always dangers involved with fishing. This is the most dangerous situation I've been in and I have been caught a few times. Having a pole back in my hands, I feel as though I've caught a strong fish and I'll just hold on. I've lost much of the feeling that a fish has caught me. A fisherman always dreams of catching a fish large enough to provide a great fight. I have now hooked such a thing and I would be greatly disappointed to cut the line unless I know I absolutely have no choice.

The movements of a swimming fish and a following canoe fell into an almost predictable pattern. The shark swam northeastward. During occasional surges, line was released. In the fish's quieter periods, the canoe drew closer.

On one occasion, when Seth woke up, he realized he was continuing to grip the pole; but the line was slack. He reeled in line rapidly until it became taut again. A tall, wide, dark fin broke through the Gulf's ghostly surface. This stealthy thing moved smoothly while circling the canoe. Is that creature hunting me now? Seth asked himself. I'm supposed to be the fisherman around here. As quickly as the fin had appeared, it vanished. Later the canoe was again pulled to the northeast.

While being led by a fish between unending layers of water and sky,

Sethrum was awed by the immensity of all things around him. His canoe and himself seemed to be the only frailties on the Gulf lit by a silver moon. An heron flew passed. It was a long way out for a shore bird. The large bird squawked once, maybe offering a greeting or sounding an alarm at seeing such an unusual sight upon the water. An orange colored sea turtle pushed upward through the water's surface. This creature reminded Seth of the timelessness of things other than himself. Small flocks of cormorants as well as egrets crossed the sky occasionally. Pale forms of terns circled overhead in a star sprinkled sky. Backs of dolphins, breaking regularly through the water's surface, caused a run on the line, rushing the canoe eastward.

I've made a mistake, Seth warned himself. I've stayed with this creature too long. I'm out too far and off course. I'm the only thing out in this vastness that doesn't belong here. I have waited too long. I'm in trouble now regardless of what I do so I might as well try to catch this large fish. Likely, I've just caught a lot o' trouble. But if I release the shark now, I will have accomplished nothing. My truck is parked on the shore to the northwest. I've been traveling more eastward, even southeast. I'm hungry and thirsty. As long as I have this fish, I at least have food even if I have to eat it raw.

Sethrum slept and was awakened by a lunge of the fish against the line. A first edge of the rising sun shot tendrils of red light along the water and across a cloud-strewn sky. Sethrum felt cold, hungry and thirsty. His muscles ached. I have pains now, he said to himself. This seems to be my way of doing things. I like trying the more difficult struggle, catching the larger fish. I could try for smaller catches; but I've hooked a great shark and I'm going to hang on. In my own mind, at least, I've passed the point of no return. I wouldn't trade many small fish for one large one. Even where women are concerned, I like to go the hard way—the long route—and find the right one. This shark is a challenge. I've caught them off islands in the Caribbean as well as along the American, Atlantic coast. This time, I'm out from the everglades with a prize so large the thing maybe has caught me. I'm not going to release such an opportunity because they don't come along often.

Deciding he had to act decisively in order to continue being the hunter instead of becoming the prey, he pulled the line sharply northward to steer the large fish back toward land. Lurching in response, the creature almost tore the pole from Seth's grip. Afterward, the shark swam more toward the north.

The sun rose slowly to become a scarlet sphere positioned above a crimson haze. Cries from terns and gulls greeted the dawn. Egrets, flying overhead, were touched by pink hues from the sun. A single cormorant flew southward.

I have no wish to hurt anything or anyone, reflected Sethrum. Fishing, though, doesn't bother me. I don't waste anything or cause any unnecessary harm. This episode will finish my shark fishing. I can't top catching a large shark by canoe. I'm now thinking less about the excitement of fishing and more about food. This shark has become my source of food. I'm also thirsty and sore along with being tired. While I have this fish, I have food. Although fishing doesn't bother me, I wouldn't hunt birds or animals. I've always thought the destruction of a fox overshadowed anything good that might come from a foxhunt.

Sethrum hauled again on the line, steering the powerful creature more to the north. A slight breeze started to stir the water, curling away strands of mist. Large waves could toss this canoe around like a leaf, Seth warned himself. I must get back to land as soon as possible. I have traveled a long way without having to do any paddling.

Ahead of the canoe, a large, dark fin sliced through the water's surface, carving a long arc before submerging again. If this contest came to a violent confrontation, I wouldn't survive long in my frail canoe, Seth told himself. I will defeat this creature by using my wits. I must be careful to not underestimate a shark's thinking ability because there's much I don't understand. In my experience, the shark has been the only fish that has deliberately tried to bite me. My fingers have been caught in the jaws of other fish; but I'm sure, each time, the fish just closed its jaws and my fingers got in the way. When I've been unhooking sharks, they have deliberately tried to bite me. The most painful bite I've had came when the shark bit my hand and I had to cut the fish's head off to get the thing to loosen its grip. Because sharks have intentionally tried to bite me, maybe this critter could decide to attack. The shark at least belongs to the sea and I don't. My journey here has come by accident. I respect those who deliberately go to the sea, particularly in small crafts, although I suppose any vessel can be considered small when compared to the power of the water. I can appreciate the courage of the Indian people in America who traveled by canoe. They even traveled to islands in the Caribbean. The Kon-Tiki expedition followed likely water routes to the Polynesian Islands.

Dolphins swam close to the canoe. Soon afterward, line screamed from the reel. The canoe rushed through cresting waves toward a dark outline of land to the north. While the fish pulled the canoe, this outline became larger and grew upon the water until there came into view the palm-topped everglades.

Pelican Moon

After the canoe had been guided into a bay, the line went slack. Seth vigorously reeled in loose line then a dark fin broke through the surface and circled the canoe.

Seth saw a worrisomely large, streamlined form move through water close to the canoe. The craft was nudged by something. Seth frantically continued to wind in line. Maybe the thing has broken lose and is out to get me, though Seth before a screaming burst of line was pulled out from the reel, almost toppling him into the water. The shark was swimming swiftly out of the bay.

Not wanting to get taken back to the Gulf, Sethrum released line then paddled furiously toward shore. When the craft grated against coral, he jumped into shallow water and started to rapidly wind in line. It came in easily until it hit the shark swimming in the opposite direction. The rod bent and the reel screamed as line was pulled away. A fin broke through the water's surface out in the bay. This fin moved steadily in a long curve heading gradually toward land.

This is the way fishing should be, Sethrum noted with satisfaction. I'm standing on something solid and the fish is in the water. The shark had its chance to catch me. Now things are back in my favor.

The final fight was short because the fish was tired. Its fin sliced along the surface and came closer to Sethrum. I would like to let this shark go, thought Seth. But I need the food.

A dark, streamlined form swirled in the water near Sethrum. When he tightened the line, the fish lunged at the surface, creating an explosion of spray. Seth pulled the line again, sending the shark into a thrashing frenzy at the water's edge. The large body gashed itself on coral. A red spray of blood mixed with the water and flowing blood quickly ended the creature's struggles.

Wading into the shallow water, Seth rinsed blood from his skin and clothes. Weary from the long struggle, he didn't immediately respond to the sight of something moving under the surface. When the jaws opened, with water splashing away from them, Seth sprang back to land and thrashed through a tangle of mangroves. Terrified, he became almost snared by trunks. His heart was pounding with a tangible fear he had not known before. Looking behind him, and saw a powerful alligator ripping meat away from the shark. Resembling pieces of tire floating on the water, other alligators moved toward the blood and food. Commencing an explosion of spraying water and writhing forms, alligators tore at the meat, taking most of it into deeper water. By pulling on the line, Seth hauled a large chunk into a thicket of mangroves.

Egrets flew across a crest of palms etched jaggedly against pink clouds above the setting sun. Silence fell with deepening hues of evening.

Sethrum sat down on fine, white sand at the base of mangroves well back from the coral shoreline. His hand shook as he removed a crumpled cigar from his jacket pocket. A flame from his lighter lit a broken end of the cigar sending a wisp of aromatic smoke drifting upward away from his face. He smoked the cigar slowly while trying to stop shaking and collect his thoughts. That Gulf is not always as friendly as it looks, he said to himself. I've almost been eaten twice during this fishing trip. I must be careful or I'm going to end up inside something's belly.

Trying to relax by smoking a broken cigar, he watched ridged backs of alligators swirling along the water's surface. A water moccasin slithered passed. I have a canoe, some equipment and food, Seth said to himself. Before

Pelican Moon

I started washing off the blood, I found that I could drink the water. It was only slightly salty so fresh water is entering this bay. I must be close to the mouth of a river. Fresh water from the everglades enters the Gulf along this shoreline.

I'm not really lost, he reasoned. I came from the west. If I paddle north, maybe I'll come to a road. I don't want to sleep on the ground because there are too many alligators around—and snakes. I must protect my canoe so I can get out o' here. I would like to sleep in an aboveground shelter; but I don't have much time. I must get busy and put together a shelter.

By tying mangrove poles together with fish line, Sethrum constructed an high platform. On this frame, he placed his canoe in an upright position. To get into the canoe easily, he made a ladder. I'll sleep in my canoe, he told himself, being pleased with his practicality. When I get time, I'll add a roof.

Seth built a campfire beside his shelter then cut steaks from the shark meat. With a long, straight piece of live oak, he carved a spear. He held it in flames of his campfire to harden this weapon, particularly its point. He also fashioned a club from the same wood. Having completed all necessary work, he used his spear to roast shark steaks over the flames.

Seth kept being disturbed by thrashing sounds coming from the area where he hung up the remaining chunk of the shark. When he checked this cache, he saw a large alligator tear loose a piece of the dwindling meat supply. The reptile took this food to the water and quickly slipped beneath the surface. Seth cut off a few sections. He carried them to his canoe to be stored with other steaks and equipment.

Being prepared for the night, he sat down on dry sand. He leaned his back against a tripod made by tieing mangrove poles together. He rested while enjoying heat from the fire. Watching its light flicker into a seemingly endless swamp, he concluded, I've saved all the meat I can look after. Alligators and snakes can have the rest of the shark. As if in reply to this thought, thrashing sounds came from the vicinity of the cache. Silence followed. A water moccasin swam through firelight glimmering on the water.

Just as Seth saw the snake, jaws shot through the surface, sending up a crest of spray, and clamped down on the serpent. The alligator's massive head twisted back and forth before submerging beneath remnant bubbles and ripples. The snake's tail flipped out of the water only to be pulled down again beneath firelight dancing on the surface. Alligators are eating well tonight, thought Sethrum as he tried to dispel his sense of unease.

After climbing the ladder, he stepped into his canoe. He stretched out almost comfortably with his back on the floor. I'll leave the ground to snakes and alligators, he told himself. I just hope they stay there. He looked up at a ghostly moon in a starlit sky. An heron flew passed the outline of the moon. A dog barked and a panther screamed from somewhere in the swamp. There's an eerie beauty in this place, Seth reflected. There are also dangers lurking everywhere. At night I sense the danger although I can't see it. I'm always watching for reptiles and they aren't my favorite critters. I relate best to animals, birds or fish. I'm drawn to wild places.

He slept until being awakened by an aircraft passing overhead. Mist in the swamp was tinted red by first rays of light from the rising sun. He climbed down from the canoe and went to check the cached meat. It was missing. In place of the meat, there stood an heron and an egret.

Having untied his canoe from the platform of poles, he removed the craft and placed it on fine sand at the water's edge. He checked his supplies including shark steaks, fishing pole, knife, spear, club, lighter and cigars. After securing his equipment, he was easing the craft over coral at the shoreline when he heard a grunt come from a clump of saw palmettos.

Shaking a long, black snake, a wild hog emerged from the palmettos. Surging with confidence after a victorious battle, this tusked boar stared at Sethrum then charged. The animal sprang forward like a released spring, with muscles rippling. Flailing hooves shot up a spray of white sand. The snake was dropped during the furious attack.

Immobilized at first by the shocking impact from seeing what he could not believe, Sethrum also had to shake off an icy grip of fear before he flashed into action to save his life with whatever was available. He grasped his spear and wedged its blunt end against coral while aiming the point at the hog. The tip slammed into the pig's upper chest or throat, knocking the animal's head and body back in a leg sprawling summersault. Seth used the club once to make sure the battle was over. The animal's struggles lessened until only its blood moved in the water.

Dazed by the fury of such an assault, Seth looked around at his surroundings. Nothing stirred as if stillness and silence had to follow such a release of wild energy. He was shocked by such an unprovoked charge. I almost got killed again, he reminded himself. I suppose, just because I happened to be standing here, my presence was a challenge to the victorious boar. There's too much uncertainty in this wilderness as to who is going to get eaten. Luckily, I'll be doing the eating this time. I now have lots of food.

He butchered the pig and placed the meat on the hide in the bow of the canoe. After easing the craft away from coral along the shoreline, Seth stepped inside, sat down in the stern and was pleased to start paddling again. Dipping his paddle into clear water, he turned the craft toward a wide opening in a verdant shoreline. When saw palmetto and palm bordered banks opened on each side, he realized he had entered the mouth of a shallow river. A slight current stirred toward the Gulf.

Beyond a curve in the river, a dog barked. This familiar sound was followed by an eerie silence broken occasionally by the gurgling of water surging against the bow or the changing and cheerful song of a mocking bird. Emerald flashes marked the flight of two parakeets. From the sun-bleached branches of a dead, slash pine, an osprey watched the passing craft. A melodious blend of birdcalls reverberated beyond winding borders of the river. Some edges of the river became lost among mangrove and cypress swamps. Riverbanks became increasingly less distinct.

After unexpectedly coming upon a point of solid ground, Seth decided to construct a camp. Knowing the shark meat would spoil if he didn't use it soon, he roasted steaks over flames of a small campfire. He savored a meal of juicy, white meat, followed by a drink of slightly cool, fresh water. Before he rested, he completed the work of butchering the boar then wrapped the meat in sea grape leaves. Leftover pieces were either left for alligators or thrown to a waiting heron and egret.

While the setting sun turned to a rose colored orb amid a purple haze, shadows lengthened and deepened in the everglades. The setting sun formed a pink trail on the river, leading from purple mist in the west to the flickering campfire.

Firelight continued to brighten in contrast to evening shadows. I enjoy the company of my main visitors, the heron and egret, reflected Seth. I'm getting more aware of the seemingly innumerable creatures linked to the Gulf. I like the sandpipers that live along the shoreline. I'm learning more about the shells such as coquinas or welks. I have to be careful to not step on any more sting rays or sea urchins. Although being speared by a sail cat's barb is very painful and a stingray's jab burns like fire, the most painful injury of them all is the shark bite. The jaws clamped on my hands with bone crushing pain. Killing the shark is the only way I've discovered to get this fish to loosen its grip. A shark will also bite intentionally. Other fish have only sunk teeth into my hands by accident. Getting a hook into my own hand was also painful, having to push the hook all the way through the skin before I could break off the barb.

The heron called once hoarsely before outstretching broad wings and flying above the river and following its shimmering route into the everglades. There's always something new to discover on a beach before each wave changes the landscape, thought Seth. I've even found encrusted coins along with fossilized bones and teeth in addition to arrowheads and pieces of pottery. Seth watched the water's surface where last rays of sunlight shone through mist before withdrawing, leaving a brief afterglow.

If I could catch minnows here, I could do some fishing, observed Sethrum. I like pinfish; although there seems to be nothing better than scaled sardines for bait.

A dog's barking brought Seth's attention back to his present circumstances. The sharp barks came at almost regular intervals and were getting closer. Campfire flames flickered light across palms silhouetted against a pink sky. Four cormorants flew through a darkening sky as the dog barked again.

Sethrum heard something splashing in shallow water upstream. A pink glow in the swamp had turned to murkiness. The next bark was very close to camp. In the generally still and silent everglades, the barking seemed to be coming from shadows just beyond the firelight. An high pitched squeal followed by a guttural growl exploded through the night's solitude.

Seth ran to get his club and spear amid a crescendo of grunts, squeals and growls mixed with the splashing of water and thrashing of brush. Walking slowly beyond the firelight, Seth peered into a thicket of saw palmettos. There was enough light for him to see that a greyhound had backed a wild hog into a furious standoff consisting of charge and counter charge. The dog moved with such speed, each action was blurred.

The hog was on the defensive; but made vicious thrusts with tusks.

At Seth's approach, the greyhound broke off a steady assault and dashed with uncanny speed toward Seth. For an instant, he was gripped by shock, not knowing what to do. The dog's muscle's bunched then released in a long jump bringing the animal onto Seth, knocking him off balance. Following this quick greeting, the greyhound swirled back to confront the hog.

The wild pig broke from its cover. Almost in the same flash of movement, the greyhound jumped and knocked over the hog. The pig tumbled, kicking up sand in a tall spray. Both animals quickly regained their stances. Like a snarling whirlwind, the hog charged Sethrum who put all his strength into swinging his club at the approaching menace. Seth's blow struck just before he was knocked to the sand. Stunned, he could see the tusks thrusting—almost feel them—when the dog attacked, drawing away the tusks. Seth swung his club again, giving the dog an opening for a neck hold, ending the battle.

Sethrum sat down. He was exhausted and sweating. Leaving the hog, the dog came over and leaned his head against Seth's shoulder. In greeting, Sethrum slapped the animal's lean sides. Friends have been forged in battle, thought Seth.

While the dog watched, the pig was pulled to camp and butchered. Leftover sections were taken to high ground away from camp to feed an assortment of critters. The dog showed no interest in the meat until the last of the shark steaks were skewered, along with pork steaks, over the fire. This roasted meat was shared equally. After stretching out on the ground, the greyhound used its front paws to anchor each steak so it could be eaten slowly.

That dog hunts hogs because he likes pork, observed Sethrum. I don't think the dog is lost. He was just hunting.

He only eats cooked meat and isn't unusually hungry. There will be an owner around somewhere and not too far away either. I should give the dog a name. I think I'll call him Swamp.

The dog rested contentedly in light from the fire. Meanwhile Sethrum built two tripod frames to hold the canoe and keep it off the ground. When the canoe was in place, Swamp slept in the bow. Seth rested in the stern. He watched the starlit sky. The moon first appeared as a red glow that lost color while ascending. Later, silver moonlight formed a tangle of patterns in the swamp. This light also brightened tendrils of mist rising from the river. One falling star flashed across the sky. Occasionally, an aircraft, accompanied by a faint sound, moved slowly passed the stars. Splashing sounds came from the area where leftover meat had been placed. A distant snarl of a panther stirred Swamp. With ears perked, he raised his head, sniffed the air and

Pelican Moon

seemed to not detect anything of particular interest. "You hunt like a panther," said Seth to the watchful dog. "Maybe you hunt with a panther."

Little sleep came to Seth during the night. Wind rattled palm fronds while rain splashed into the canoe. The bailing can removed most of the water.

Seth was awakened at dawn by Swamp's barking. He had cornered something under the canoe. Sethrum looked down and saw a water moccasin striking at swamp. The dog was a match for the snake's speed. Each thrust forward of the snake's head was met by a rapid retreat followed instantly by an attack with jaws snapping at any loose coil. When Seth hit the reptile with the spear, Swamp got a grip on a coil then shook the serpent, quickly killing it. Seth used his spear to throw the ropelike form toward the ridged back of an alligator resting in the water. The alligator swirled with surprising speed. Large jaws clamped down on the snake and thrashed back and forth before submerging, leaving behind only a rippled surface that gradually became calm again.

Along with rays of sunlight, serenity seeped into the morning. The river's surface reflected overhanging foliage, mixing deceptive images with real forms, creating a duality that was so much a part of the swamp. An heron and egret flew into camp to get pieces of meat. Cormorants and terns crossed the sky as a rising sun warmed the morning and burned off mist. Seth roasted pork for himself and Swamp.

When Seth slipped his canoe into the water, he learned immediately that Swamp was experienced with such crafts. The dog went directly to the bow and stayed there. He watched the river with its emerald colored shoreline. He also sniffed the air, checking intriguing traces of scents. Accustomed to traveling by canoe, Sethrum paddled rhythmically along the river of slightly

Pelican Moon

cool, fresh water. Flashes of green marked the flights of parakeets. Carrying a large snake, an eagle flew above the treetops. Minnows rippled the water as a large fish's tail broke through the surface then submerged again.

Sethrum continued paddling his canoe upstream between verdant banks covered by a profusion of plant life. Seeing no suitably dry place along the banks where he could pull his canoe onto the land to stop for a rest, he served a snack in the canoe. Both man and dog dined on previously roasted pork. Afterward, the craft proceeded northward along the river, gliding through patches of shade provided by overhanging foliage.

Seth stopped paddling so he could listen more carefully to mockingbirds singing among a canopy of live oaks. Occasionally, amid a background of birdcalls, he heard someone singing an Indian song.

TWO

SIHOKI

When Sethrum Moon's canoe was close to the western riverbank, Swamp jumped from the bow and swam to the land. Turning the canoe more toward the shore, Seth paddled in pursuit, passing a stand of cypress trees.

He proceeded to a sandy section of the riverbank. Back from this sandy area, on high ground, there was a majestic live oak. Its outstretched branches gave the tree an horizontal shape which was offset by downward sloping Spanish moss. Ponderous branches provided shade for two structures made of palm logs topped by roofs constructed with thatched, palmetto fronds. One of the buildings had two stories. The other structure featured a central cooking fire.

After stepping onto the sandy shore, Seth pulled his craft up beside a dugout canoe. Following a well-worn path on the riverbank, Swamp ran toward Seth. Seeing something move beside him, Seth turned just as the dog jumped up in greeting and both man and dog fell in a sand-spraying tumble. "You silly mutt," exclaimed Seth, resting on his back, looking up at the slender dog. "I'm sure pleased you're friendly."

Sethrum stood up. He shook sand from his clothes then removed a large piece of pork from the canoe. Carrying this food, he followed Swamp as the dog hurried along the path.

The trail led to a cooking structure where a woman was working. She had a rounded shape and wore a long, colorful dress. Lines on her face were not deeply grooved. Her eyes sparkled. "My dog knows you," she said in greeting.

"That's a good sign. A dog is good judge of character—and so am I." She continued stirring a mixture in a pot. From this cooking, Seth detected a tantalizing aroma of fish stew.

"We met in the swamp—down the river," replied Seth. "Your dog was hunting hogs. I was fishing for sharks."

"His name is Hog Hunter, or just Hunter," replied the woman. "Hog Hunter's friend is welcome here," she added while pouring a cup of coffee then giving it to Seth. Having refilled her own cup, she ladled stew into a wooden bowl. She gave this bowl to Seth, serving the steaming mixture with a silver spoon. He sat down on a bench and tasted the stew. It had vegetable flavors mingled with a mild taste of fish. The coffee was also good. "Great cooking," exclaimed Seth. "Thanks for the stew and coffee," he added. "They're both delicious. I've been without a really good meal for a long time."

Removing a piece of roasted meat from his pocket, Seth gave this food to Hunter. The dog stretched out on sandy ground beside the bench where Seth was sitting. Holding the meat between his front paws, Hunter ate the food slowly and contentedly. "What have you given Hunter?" she asked.

"Roasted pork," answered Seth. "Hunter caught it. I roasted it. I knew the dog came here to visit someone so I brought a package of pork with me. Picking up a leaf-wrapped bundle from the bench, Seth gave this package to the woman as he explained, "This is fresh pork, caught by Hunter."

"Thanks," said the woman, accepting the food. She placed it on a table beside the fire. "Do you wrap everything in sea grape leaves?" she asked, smiling and revealing particularly white teeth.

"Only fresh pork," he replied.

"Hunter only goes after pigs," explained the woman. "I wouldn't let him hunt everything. I like all things, including pigs; however, Hunter needs the interest and exercise. He also keeps the wild pigs alert and that's good for them. My brother thinks I should let Hunter chase pigs and allow him to give up racing."

"Hunter's a racer?" asked Sethrum, surprised. "I know all greyhounds are fast; but I don't think of them as all being racers."

"Hunter's one of the best," stated the woman. "As far as I'm concerned, he is the best."

"I'm Sethrum Moon, or just Seth," he said.

"I'm Sihoki Panther," replied the woman, refilling their cups with dark, flavorful coffee. "My brother's name is Will. His Indian name is Yaha Chatee. We are of the panther clan. We are Seminoles."

Reaching into his pocket, Seth removed a piece of stone and gave it to Sihoki, saying, "I found that on the beach west of here. It's an arrowhead, tip of a spearhead or the point of a knife. You can have that stone because it possibly belongs to your ancestors—or the people, who were here before them, the Tocobagas. Years ago, I found a fossilized shark's tooth. An Indian person had drilled an hole in it and used it as an amulet. I wear it sometimes."

Turning the intricately chipped and partly eroded relic in her hands, she said, "Thanks for returning our property. Much of our culture is returning. This is an arrowhead. We have others like it in our museum. I might keep this arrowhead or put it in with the others. This land is our history."

"Thank you for the stew," said Seth, putting his empty bowl along with the spoon on the table. "Stew's delicious. So's the coffee. Thanks for your hospitality."

"Some people think we're not hospitable," she replied. "Depends on who comes calling. Hunter thinks you're all right."

"Could I roast some pork for you?" asked Seth.

"Okay," she replied. "Hunter likes pork also," she added.

Seth walked to his canoe and returned with three, pork steaks skewered on his spear. Hunter watched closely while the meat roasted. Oil dripped into flames and sizzled. Steam shot from the meat as it turned golden before becoming brown.

When Sihoki brought two plates, along with knives and forks, Seth placed a steak on each plate. He cooled the third steak with water then gave this meat to Hunter. The dog stretched out on the ground and, holding the meat between his front paws, he ate slowly. Having added salt and pepper to their steaks, Sihoki and Seth savored this food along with more coffee. "You live here all the time?" asked Seth.

"Yes," she replied. "I'm here much of the time. I like the old ways better than the new. Of course, new things can be added to our traditions to keep them modern like other cultures. The Seminoles are made up of the early Indian nations who lived in Florida together with the Creeks who came south."

She gave Hunter the last part of her steak, sipped coffee and said, "My particular ancestors were Creek and Tocobaga. The Tocobaga people fought the Spanish invaders of Florida. Members of the Creek Confederacy came south because of pressure from American colonists. Andrew Jackson defeated the Creeks at Horseshoe Bend. He invaded Florida, defeating the Seminoles and Spanish. Afterward, the United States purchased Florida from Spain. Of course, in my opinion, Spain didn't own the land. The United States actually purchased Spain's claim to this area."

After Seth gave the remainder of his steak to Hunter, Sihoki continued to say, "Today the United States is a great country. This country is great enough to acknowledge that mistakes were made in the past and to have learned from those mistakes. One of our worst enemies in the government was President Andrew Jackson. He wanted the Indian people of the United States to move to Oklahoma. Many Indian people went there. The Seminoles who successfully resisted removal are here today in Florida. Some Cherokees managed to escape the same removal policy. They live today in the Smoky Mountains. My brother's wife comes from there. They have an home in the mountains. My home is here. This is an old, village site. I found pieces of pottery in the sand. Some were marked with an interesting, pelican design. Now I use this design on my pottery. In the north, I have a friend who also does pottery work and applies the pelican imprint. You will meet her some day, I think. I use pottery bowls for much of my cooking. I talk too much. Tell me more about how you met Hunter."

"I helped him catch a wild hog," answered Seth.

"Yeah," she exclaimed. "That's the way to become Hunter's friend. He loves to hunt hogs. He's a real hunter—like a panther. I once saw him traveling with a panther. Hunter started chasing pigs when I first brought him here. He was just a pup the day he tackled his first hog. I had to help with the kill. After I supported Hunter in that fight, we became pals. I don't dislike pigs. I have respect for all parts of life. Hunter and I just happen to like roast pork and there are lots o' pigs around this area."

"I guess Hunter stayed with me because I also helped him," said Seth.

"You've made a friend," confirmed Sihoki. "Would you like more stew?"

"No thanks," he replied. "I'm full."

"Coffee?" she asked.

"Okay," he answered before she refilled his cup.

"Have you wondered why I had extra food and coffee prepared, although I was here alone?" she asked.

"No, not really," he said. "Although, come to think of it, you seemed to have food for someone else who was already here somewhere, or you were expecting company."

"Did you wonder why I invited you to stay?" she asked.

"No," he replied. "I suppose being Hunter's friend helped me." For the first time, Seth started thinking about how easily he had been accepted into this camp.

"Do you think I let Hunter pick my visitors?" she asked.

"No, not entirely," he answered. These questions were making him feel

Pelican Moon

uneasy. I wonder what this woman's getting at, he thought.

Her face brightened. She looked directly at him. Her eyes had a new fire in them. "I saw a vision," she said. "In this vision, Hunter brought here a man who would reenter the spirit world and be shown things very few people see. I saw myself helping you along your journey."

Shocked by what she had said, backed by the way he had been accepted into the camp, as if he had been expected, he said, "You talk about the spirit world…. Am I going to die out here?"

"No," she answered. "The spirit world is here now. We just don't remember it, or see it, all the time."

A mix of nervousness and excitement stirred through Seth, causing him to take a fresh look at the surrounding swamp with its tranquil river flowing to the Gulf. Patches of shade, from overhanging oaks, patterned the water. A broad-winged heron flew above the stream, moving out of view beyond moss-draped, oak foliage.

"America is a modern nation," said Sihoki who also watched the river. "We have all the conveniences; yet we continue to have wilderness—places where the land has not been changed or, as they say, developed. We still have traditional homelands and heritages of the Indian people. Andrew Jackson's removal bill was only passed by one vote. Davy Crockett from Tennessee voted against the bill and so did many others. Although mistakes are made, many people are well informed. The Seminoles and other Indian nations have kept their traditions. The longevity of our citizenship does not lessen it."

"Fortunately, the wilderness continues to be part of this land," observed Sethrum. "Today, we have bears and panthers although there are less of them."

"The wilderness continues with all its beauty," agreed Sihoki.

"Hog Hunter is part wild," noted Seth. "He hunts with panthers."

"Do you ever go to the dog races?" asked Sihoki with an added sparkle in her eyes.

"A few times," answered Seth.

"Next time you go, you should bet on your friend over there," she said, looking at the dog resting near the other building.

"I thought dogs needed special training to run in races," replied Seth.

"Hunter has had the training," confirmed Sihoki. "My brother, Will, looks after the dogs. He supplies dogs to a kennel that sends them to the track. The kennel trains many of its greyhounds, but not all of them. Will works for the kennel. He raises pups. Hog Hunter is the best dog Will ever had. Because Hunter has become so much of a pet, my brother would like to take him out of the races. Hunter, being so much of a friend, has also become a little too independent. Sometimes, though, that dog can run like the wind. At other times, he just can't be bothered. Racing can be hard on an animal, so a dog shouldn't race too long. Will wants to retire Hunter and I don't want him to quit too soon. I know Hunter has good races left in him and he should run them before he finishes. I think such a theory also applies to people. We should never quit too soon. Like sled dogs up north, some greyhounds love to run. Hunter loves to race and chase hogs. However, as I said before, he has become a little too independent."

Sihoki poured more coffee before she said, "Hog Hunter is more of an hunter than a racer. A racer is fast; but an hunter is strong and steady. During a race, other dogs can't knock Hunter over or out of the way. Many races are determined at the first turn. The dogs that don't get knocked off course can win the race. Hunter is also at his very best in wet weather. He loves a swamp. If the weather is wet, and dogs on the inside track are fast, bet them to win because being on the inside is an advantage in bad weather. If Hog Hunter is in the same race, bet him to come third and you will win a lot of money on the trifecta. If you win, stop betting, because, in gambling, over the long run, you will lose."

"Thanks for the tips," replied Seth. "I'll try them on a wet day."

"I would like to go back to my house now," said Sihoki abruptly. "Are you ready to travel upstream?"

"Yes," he answered as he stood up. Returning the cup to Sihoki, he said, "Thanks for the coffee and stew."

"We can each take a canoe up the river," said Sihoki. "When we get back, my brother will give you a ride to help you get where you want to go."

"That's great," he exclaimed. "Thanks."

Seth helped her carry cooking equipment and other supplies to her dugout. Afterward, he pushed her canoe into the water before preparing his own canoe. Hog Hunter jumped into the dugout and sat in the bow.

Sihoki moved her dugout forward by using a push-pole. Seth paddled his craft beside the dugout and both canoes proceeded steadily along the stream. The travelers passed between walls of greenery. Overhead, there was a canopy of branches and foliage. Birds darted among branches draped with Spanish moss. A snake dropped beside Seth's canoe then slithered toward a vine-covered bank.

The water trail brought the two canoes to an outcropping of white sand in front of a one story, wooden house. It had a spacious, screened veranda facing the river. Dogs barked from enclosures behind the building. Hog Hunter barked in reply.

The canoes were met by a tall, lean man with short, black, although graying, hair. His eyes were brown. His large, strong hands moved the canoes with a quickness and skill of a man who is

Pelican Moon

always working at something. "He's the one?" the man asked Sihoki.

"Yes," she answered. "He's Sethrum Moon."

"Pleased to meet you," said Seth before stepping out of his canoe and shaking hands with the man.

"I told you about my brother, Will," said Sihoki to Seth. She had left her canoe and Will pulled it farther onto the bank.

"You train dogs?" Seth asked Will.

"Yes," he replied as he lifted a package from the dugout. "Come inside." Seth carried other equipment from Sihoki's canoe then followed the two people and Hunter to the house.

Seth was taken into a building that was a practical, clean home, having a fireplace. "I like the fireplace," observed Seth.

"I learned to like them in the Smoky Mountains," replied Will. When Seth saw the rifle leaning against the wall next to the doorway, Will said, "I feed bears back in the swamp but I don't like them in my kitchen."

After each person sat down on a chair in the spacious, living room, Seth asked Will, "You enjoy training dogs?"

"Oh yes," he exclaimed with an extra glow in his eyes. "I raise dogs for pets and racing. I would like to see Hog Hunter retire. I think he, like me, is getting too old for racing."

"There are a lot o' good races left in both o' you," countered Sihoki. Smiling, she added, "Although, I'm not so sure about you."

"You might worry about me," said Will to Sihoki. "I'm only worried about Hog Hunter." To Seth, Will said, "I work for a kennel that supplies dogs to the track. I'll give you Hog Hunter's schedule for racing. If the weather is bad, Hunter will do well. He likes water."

"He helped me catch some pork," said Seth as he stood up. "I'm going to get something. I'll be right back." When

Seth left the house, Hunter accompanied him. They both walked to the canoe. Seth obtained a bundle of pork and carried this package to the house. Giving the bundle to Sihoki, Seth said, "Hunter and I have some more pork for you."

"Thanks," she said, accepting the food. Looking at Will, she said, "Seth and Hunter have been giving us pork." She carried the meat to the kitchen while Will started a fire in the fireplace. Afterward, he went to the kitchen then returned carrying tall glasses filled with beer. "Like a beer?" he asked, giving Seth a glass.

"Thanks," replied Seth accepting the cold, damp glass. Each person sat down again on comfortable chairs. A fragrance of wood smoke drifted in the room while a fire flickered and snapped in the fireplace.

Sethrum sipped the mild tasting beer and felt very contented. The Panthers' hospitality was warm and natural. Seth felt very much at home in their house. Will and his sister, Sihoki, had kind faces.

"I've made money betting on Hog Hunter," explained Will. "He's such a friend to me, I would like to retire him as a present for him. Sihoki thinks he should run as long as there's a good race left in him. She also said you probably need a ride. Later, I'll put your canoe on my truck."

"That would be appreciated," replied Seth. "My truck is on a side road west of here."

"After you have had time to rest, we could have a look for your truck," said Will.

"My trucks probably quite a way up the road," explained Seth. "Maybe we should go any time you're ready," he added, standing up. "Thanks for the beer," he said while he and Will walked to the kitchen. They both put their empty beer glasses on a counter beside the sink. Sihoki also took her class to the counter, saying, "I'll clean the dishes later."

Leaving the building, Hunter ran ahead of the three people as they walked to the canoes. Sethrum helped Will load the canoe onto a truck parked beside the house.

After using ropes to tie the canoe to the truck, Will sat on the driver's seat. Beside him, sat Hunter. Sihoki had a little room between the dog and Seth who was next to the door. "Gets a little crowded in here sometimes," Sihoki said to Seth. "Hunter thinks he's entitled to be beside Will."

A setting sun painted the swamp with scarlet hues while the truck proceeded westward. By the time the vehicle turned onto a sandy side road leading to Seth's truck, the landscape was patterned by ghostly light from a silver moon.

Will and Seth moved the canoe to Seth's vehicle. With the work completed, Will and Sihoki were eager to return home. "Thank you for all of your help," said Sethrum before he opened the driver's door of his truck.

"Come and see us again anytime," replied Sihoki.

"Remember Hunter's races—his last races," added Will before he started driving along the sandy road leading to the highway. Upon reaching the highway, he turned eastward. Sethrum drove toward the west and went back to his room at the Blue Heron Motel.

THREE

HOG HUNTER

At the Blue Heron Motel, Sethrum Moon sat on a chair located on the balcony in front of his room. He snacked on pistachios and sipped beer while he watched the shoreline where waves crashed against the beach, sending water surging up along the sand, only to withdraw again in an hissing rush back to the Gulf. Sandpipers ran to look for food in the flowing turbulence of each retreating wave.

Clouds, moving out of the west, gradually blocked much sunlight, darkening hues of the landscape. Adding a flash of white to the greens, yellows and blues of the shoreline, an egret flew to the beach and watched the rushing waves. An heron added its stately form to the top of a chimney on neighboring condominiums. Backs of passing dolphins periodically broke through the water's surface as clouds continued to erase light from the sunset. A breeze rattled palm fronds. The weather forecast calls for rain tomorrow, noted Seth before he opened another can of beer. I must go to the track tomorrow because Hog Hunter is scheduled to be racing. This race could be the last for Hunter, according to Will Panther.

Next morning, the breeze had stiffened to a wind that sent waves crashing along the beach. Wearing a swimsuit, Seth walked into the water. I probably won't get any minnows when the water's so rough, he thought as he waited for an hissing wave to pass. He threw out his minnow net then pulled it to shore to unload a shining harvest of scaled sardines, also known as whitebait.

Seth threw some minnows to gulls clamoring overhead. He also fed his more solitary, hunting friends, the heron and egret. Lastly, he baited his fishing line with a large sardine. He waded out again into the water then threw the line, weighted by an heavy, sand sinker, as far out as it would go over the cresting waves.

Returning to shore, he put his fishing pole in a sand spike and was about to tighten the line when the pole bent like a strand of grass blown in the wind. The reel screamed as line was pulled toward the Gulf. Seth grabbed the pole. He first tightened the tension on the line so it wouldn't all be torn away by a large, fighting fish. It was surging toward deeper water. Line continued to be removed from the reel, although at a slower rate. Again Seth checked the tension. It was as tight as the line could take without breaking. Far out from shore, a large fish thrashed at the surface. The pole continued to bend wildly. Line was taken out in spurts although some was also retrieved. Gradually, more line was being wound in than was getting pulled away until the fish splashed close to shore. A shark maybe, thought Seth as he hauled on the line causing a dark, streamlined form to thrash at the water's edge. A cobia, Seth told himself. Keeping the line taut, he ran to the struggling fish and pulled it onto the sand.

Sethrum filleted the cobia. Holding strips of meat between his fingers, Seth fed the egret until this fisherman flew with the wind and soared happily above the shoreline. The heron could swallow much larger chunks and took longer to fill. Finally though, this fisherman was also content. Outstretching broad wings and issuing a departing squawk, this stately bird climbed into the wind and moved away toward the shelter of palms and buildings. Pelicans soared overhead. One bird swooped to the beach where Seth was filleting. He threw a chunk of meat toward the waiting bird. The pelican moved awkwardly on land although the yellow eyes were alert. They didn't miss any signs that might lead to a meal of fish. The pelican returned to the sky above the wave crested water, leaving Seth alone on the beach. Unused remnants of the fish were in a bag and would be placed in a garbage bin. Sethrum placed fillets in a second, plastic bag.

He watched pelicans diving for fish a short distance out from shore. Usually, a fish was caught with each dive. Gulls often stood on the pelican's head or back and tried to steal the catch. Black, streamlined cormorants flew across the sky and sandpipers tirelessly ran to check water withdrawing along the sand after each wave crashed against the beach.

Seth took the fillets to his room. He froze most of the meat. To prepare a meal, using the rest of the fillets, he usually liked to shake them in a plastic bag containing corn meal. However, he had been experimenting with a different batter and decided to try the new mixture. After placing one quarter cup of flour in a bowl, he added one half tablespoon of baking powder followed by one half teaspoon of salt, one half teaspoon sugar, two teaspoons of vegetable oil, one quarter cup of water and one egg. He stirred this batter, coated the fillets then fried them to prepare golden, crispy, coated fillets of cobia. Garnished simply with salt, pepper and vinegar, Sethrum enjoyed an excellent fish dinner.

Following a fine meal, Seth threw pieces of bread to a raucous flock of gulls. Some gulls, along with a crow and a grackle took pieces of food from Seth's fingers. Sparrows came to get small pieces of bread placed on the floor of the balcony. The birds are always watching my room, observed Seth. They know where they can get food. They also know a friend from an enemy. Kids are feared because they throw things at birds. Cats are always a menace. The heron isn't on the chimney because the wind is too strong. The heron and egret are probably resting somewhere along the inland waterways.

Sethrum sat on one of the chairs located on his balcony. After lighting a cigar, he watched smoke being carried eastward by a wind that was bringing more clouds and likely rain. Pelicans passed overhead. They drifted effortlessly with the wind. People have difficulty recognizing individual birds, reflected Seth. However, birds identify people as individuals. The heron and egret clearly recognize me as an individual and, like dogs, have started following me around. Birds, animals and fish are smarter than people realize. Plants also react well to kind care.

When I'm fishing, the heron and egret stay quite close to me. They even watch the fishing pole and get ready to receive eatable fish. Both birds will walk or fly away if a stranger approaches them. They can also spot me on a crowded beach and follow either by walking or flying. Seth smoked a cigar slowly until he decided to go to the races.

He left the motel and was approaching his truck when he saw the rounded tips of large jaws protruding from between metal bars of a drainage grate. Upon walking closer, Seth was amazed to see the head of a large alligator. It must've crawled into the drainage system at a young age then grew too large to get back through holes in the grates, reasoned Seth. I'll lift the cover and let the critter escape. Seth removed the metal cover then stepped out of the way as a large alligator climbed out of the opening and scurried out of view among sea grapes and tall grass.

Pelican Moon

Seth quickly slipped the cover over the hole. He was walking to his truck when he heard a rustling noise. Looking toward the source of this sound, he saw the alligator shaking a large rattlesnake. I think I'm starting to appreciate alligators, Seth said to himself before he opened the door of his truck. Sitting on the driver's seat, he started the engine and enjoyed the rush of fresh air coming through open windows during the trip to the track.

At the racetrack, Sethrum bought a program. It listed Hog Hunter as being number four, in the second race. Seth walked to the third floor of the grandstand. He selected a chair beside the isle. From here, he had a full view of the track. A steady breeze bent back palm fronds. Rain continued to soak a track that was already wet.

Leadouts walked eight dogs for the first race, giving Seth time to consider Sihoki's advice. Dogs on the inside track have an advantage in bad weather, she had said. According to the program, the dogs to be running on the inside of the track were listed as being particularly fast. Sihoki had said Hog Hunter was inconsistent; yet would be at his best in wet weather. Dogs, numbered one and three, running on the inside of the track, are listed as being faster than Hog Hunter, noted Seth. I think I'll put all my betting money on two trifecta bets arranged one, three, four and three, one, four. Dogs one and three will do well on the inside while Hunter will break out of the pack to come in third. I'm not letting down Hog Hunter because he isn't listed as being as fast as the other dogs running on the inside of the track. However, he will do well today because of the wet track.

The band was playing for the first race when Seth returned to his chair, having made his bets. He had a large cup of draft beer along with two trifecta tickets for the second race. Strains of music from the band were

Pelican Moon

joined by shrill barks from dogs in their boxes. The band stopped playing. The dogs became silent. When a mechanical rabbit approached the boxes, dogs flashed in pursuit like one, swiftly moving creature with many legs and heads. Rounding the clubhouse turn, the creature bunched together before five dogs tumbled off stride, falling in a splashing bundle of flailing legs and heads.

After the fall, dog numbered two took the lead, followed by numbers one and six. The other five dogs stretched out behind. The first dogs to cross the finish line were one, then two and six. The trifecta paid seventeen hundred dollars for a two-dollar bet. If the weather has a similar affect on the second race, thought Sethrum, Hog Hunter could win a lot o' money for his friends. I'll place bets, the same as my numbers, for Sihoki and Will because I'm betting with their information.

Having placed four additional bets, Seth purchased another large cup of beer before returning to the same chair. He got back to his place in time to see leadouts walking eight dogs. There's Hunter, Seth said to himself. He has an interesting life. A few days ago he was hunting pigs in the swamp. He's number four. He'll think he's back in the swamp on this track.

Finishing his beer quickly to try to relax, Seth ran to get another. When he got back to his chair, the dogs were in their boxes. Shrill barks mixed with music from the band. I know that people generally always lose at gambling, Seth said to himself. This occasion, for me, is just one rare shot, a calculated adventure. Sometimes we have to take a risk, go a little farther, work a little harder, or attempt something that might be out o' reach. We'll never know what could've been achieved if we don't try. When I approach the end of my life, I don't want to look back and see a lot o' things I should have done differently, or should have at least tried.

Silence followed the movement of the rabbit until, after the rabbit, there rushed a blur of massed bodies, legs and heads. At the clubhouse turn, four dogs swirled out and fell behind a leading group splashing along the track.

Number one is the lead dog, Seth told himself as he tensed with excitement. His heart pounded. He almost could not believe what he was seeing. A chilling touch of reality tingled through him when he saw that number two was the second dog, followed by numbers four and three. Why don't I listen to people? Seth asked himself. Sihoki told me to bet on the inside dogs and that would include dog, numbered two. In this race, though, two wasn't supposed to be fast.

While Seth watched, feeling both spellbound and worried, the dogs flashed around the last turn as one, three, two and four. Come on Hunter, Seth said to himself.

Hunter and the dog, numbered two, ran side by side across the finish line, behind one and three. There's a delayed, photo finish, noted Seth in growing anguish. At least I have a chance. Until I've lost, I can win. He checked his tickets that were marked one, three and four. Then to his amazement, there appeared, almost too easily, on the board, the same numbers, one, three and four.

I can't believe it, Seth exclaimed to himself. It all seems so easy when the numbers are right. This almost can't happen and likely would never occur twice; however I think this has happened now, he thought while staring at his tickets. I'll savor the moment and not rush to the betting areas.

After most people had come and gone, leaving more losing tickets scattered, like leaves, on the floor, Seth walked to the second floor, betting area. He was thinking there could still be a mistake involved somewhere. Maybe he had the wrong race—or wrong day. When he received the money, he could not believe he had won so much for himself as well as for Sihoki and Will.

Seth left the building. No one seemed to be following him. Upon reaching his truck, he got inside and locked the doors before starting the motor and driving out of the parking lot. Turning on to the highway, he relaxed somewhat once he felt he was in the anonymity of traffic.

Back at the motel, he put the winnings for Sihoki and Will into separate packets. He slept restlessly until first rays of sunlight touched the balcony. An egret waited on the balcony's railing. An heron watched from the beach. Seth threw pieces of fillets to both birds then he took his fishing pole and minnow net to the beach.

After sharing netted minnows with the heron and egret along with a few terns and gulls, Sethrum waded passed a sting ray and hurled his baited line as far out as he could send it. He returned to the beach, slipped the pole's handle into a sand spike then reeled in a little line to keep it taut.

The first fish caught was a ladyfish. It was sectioned to feed waiting birds including pelicans that were eventually driven off by the heron. The second fish bent the pole sharply while taking out line. When the departing line turned toward a buoy marking a crab trap, Seth tightened the tension on the reel, slowing the loss of line. Gradually the fighting fish was pulled toward shore then onto the beach. Seth was pleased to have caught a beautifully streamlined Spanish mackerel.

After catching a small ladyfish, Sethrum used this fish for bait. He walked to his truck, unloaded his canoe and used it to take the baited line a long way out from the shore. He was paddling back to shore when he saw in the water the slowly passing, dark form of a manatee. On shore, Seth's constant companions, the heron and egret, closely watched all Seth's actions.

Seth placed the pole in the sand spike. He sat on an eroded bank of sand then observed his fishing pole as well as the rest of the shoreline. The heron and egret waited patiently for the line to move.

Sethrum found the Gulf to be endlessly interesting. Far out from shore, he saw the rugged outline of a sea turtle's head break through the water's surface. In addition to the dark head, there was some orange coloring of the turtle's body. As quickly as this large form appeared, it submerged and vanished from view. Near the same area, two dolphins splashed at the surface, either playing or feeding. Along the beach, sandpipers ran to check water rushing back to the Gulf after each wave crashed onto the sand. Pelicans glided overhead, vigilantly patrolling the water for fish. We're all watching for fish, thought Sethrum after he lit a cigar. Fish are at the center of activities along the Gulf. The patterns of life are fascinating to watch. I never get tired of observing the shoreline. The sounds of the birds and waves are, to me, very restful.

The cresting rush of each wave toward the beach was followed by the crashing impact of the water hitting and surging along the sand then withdrawing back to the Gulf to be followed immediately by another thundering of a foaming line of water hitting the beach. Endlessly, the waves crashed against the beach and then withdrew. Gulls cried while wheeling overhead. This is my home, reflected Sethrum as he watched a tendril of smoke from his cigar get carried away by the breeze. I find rest and peace here at the beach. The sounds of the waves hitting the sand form a calming rhythm.

Pelican Moon

Everyone's after fish. There are lots o' charter boats out today. They're out farther and moving around. They must not be catching anything. Sails are slanted against the horizon, marking the courses of a few sailboats. They must be catching a stronger wind than I'm getting here. I could watch this shoreline endlessly. There's always something happening and changing. I like the water's pulse of life. Usually everything happens restfully although sometimes there are explosions of activities. Sometimes the ocean gets so active with hurricanes and tornadoes that people have to evacuate the coast. But the usual routines of natural events calm the mind. People can mow their lawns and trim bushes beside the Gulf; but these trimmings don't diminish the water's wildness. Likely, the trimmings of people, by providing a contrast, accentuate the fact that the ocean is a wilderness and it laps right up to the shore where people walk. People should be as careful here as they must be in a forested wilderness. I've been wading in this water and have been passed by a large shark's fin cutting through the surface close to my legs. I've experienced the burning pain of being speared by a stingray. I've also been speared by a catfish and bitten by a shark. The Gulf is a wilderness that laps along the shore for the interest of people who are drawn to the sea. The Gulf is wild and brings wildness to everything the water touches. There are also, of course, areas of wilderness on the land. I wonder what Sihoki meant when she said I would learn things in the spirit world that most people don't see.

The fishing rod bent sharply as line screamed from the reel. Seth grabbed the pole and felt the weight of a struggling fish pulling line into deeper water. The heron and egret watched the action closely. Pelicans soared overhead, passing a fin cutting through

Pelican Moon

waves out from shore. Gradually less line was released. Line was rewound while a struggling form veered toward the land. Sea gulls cried and wheeled through an azure sky. Above the water, cormorants flew in close formation.

The shark thrashed over a sandbar, hit deeper water bordering the beach then tried a last rush for freedom. Seth hauled on the line, sending the fish into splashing frenzy before a long, twisting form was pulled onto the sand.

People who had been watching, along with the birds, all received a share of the shark. The sea is a source of food for just about everything, thought Sethrum as he carried steaks to his room. After taking care of the meat, he returned to the beach to get his equipment. The two birds followed him back to the motel.

Seth had just placed his canoe on the truck when he noticed the heron watching something in grass next to the motel.

The bird's neck snaked forward and the long, sharp beak caught a lizard in a solid grip. Just as quickly, the lizard was swallowed. The heron didn't need that lizard, thought Seth, considering the loss of the lizard to be unnecessary.

Upon returning to his room, Seth watched the shoreline while he dined on fried, shark steak. Following this meal, he went to the beach. He stepped into the water, crossed the sandbar then walked beside the bar. Stingrays slithered away at his approach. Along the sandy bottom, there were innumerable shells such as welks, coquinas, olives, oysters and scallops along with fossilized bones and sharks' teeth.

During Sethrum's walk to check shells, gliding pelicans continued their constant quest for fish. Scaled sardines and glass minnows retreated through greenish blue water. Forms of larger fish lurked in darker depths.

Sandpipers were always busy along the shoreline.

In addition to the shells, fish and birds, Sethrum noted the constantly changing hues of the water. He kept walking until, on shore, beside a side road, he saw an heron standing on top of a seafood restaurant. That must be a good place to eat, Seth said to himself. An heron should know.

Upon entering the building and sitting on one of many unoccupied chairs next to wooden tables, Sethrum asked for beer and a few pieces of raw fish.

"Raw fish?" asked the waitress, her eyes focusing on him seriously.

"Yes," he answered. "It's for a friend. Do you have small pieces of unfrozen fish?"

"Yes," she said. "How much would you like?"

"Enough for a meal," he replied.

"You want the fish wrapped to take out?" she asked.

"Yes," he said.

"Okay," she replied before walking to the kitchen. She returned in a short time, carrying a small, butcher-wrapped bundle along with a glass of beer. Placing these items on the table in front of Seth, she returned to some work she had been doing behind a long, wooden counter.

Sethrum added a dash of salt to the beer then drank it steadily until he had drained the glass. He savored the salty, thirst-quenching, cold drink. He asked for another and finished it almost as rapidly. After leaving a tip on the table, he paid his bill and stepped outside where he was watched by the heron. Taking the pieces of fish from the paper, Seth threw them onto the roof. With wings outstretched, the bird scrambled for the food, sending each piece, one at a time, through a snakelike neck to a seemingly vast stomach. Gulls stole a few pieces although most went down the long neck. When cries of gulls grew to a shrill clamor, the heron squawked loudly then flew toward the beach. Watching the large bird's graceful departure, Sethrum thought, I must leave too. I have to deliver the money to Sihoki and Will. I also have to return to the north so I can get back to work.

Seth walked to his motel room. Like an elegantly carved ornament, the egret stood on the balcony's railing. The heron topped the chimney of the adjacent building. Having made up his mind, Seth worked quickly to prepare his equipment for a journey that would take him first to visit Will and Sihoki then north to his work.

The changing melody of a mockingbird's song accompanied Seth while he packed his equipment in his truck. He left the motel and turned southward on an almost deserted highway. Flashes of green hues marked the flight of parakeets as they flew in front of the truck on their way to cabbage palms bordering the roadside. Strains of mockingbirds' songs occasionally entered the truck's open windows during the trip to the everglades home of Sihoki and Will Panther.

Finding the house deserted, Sethrum unloaded his canoe and slipped it into the river's dark, cool water. He stepped into the familiar craft, sat down and started paddling along the old, water trail of the Seminoles. Listening to the slight gurgling sounds of the craft moving through the water, he thought, I wonder what Will, Sihoki and the spirit world have to do with me. Sihoki knew I would be visiting her. She said I was on a special kind of a journey. The river has not changed much through time. I enjoy finding such places. I can travel this river and see what others before me have seen. Maybe some of Will and Sihoki's ancestors, the Tocobagas, came this way when they were escaping from the Spaniards. Creeks would also have canoed along here in

Pelican Moon

addition to other Indian nations from the north.

Accompanied by his thoughts, Seth soon arrived at the thatched chickees of Sihoki. Smoke was coming from the cooking fire. Seeing Seth, Sihoki left the fire and walked to the riverbank as the canoe was sliding onto the sand. "You're late," she said, smiling. "There's coffee and stew."

"You haven't been expecting me again, have you?" asked Seth caught off guard again by her apparent awareness of what he was doing. He stepped out of his craft then pulled it onto the sand. Standing up, he noted Sihoki's attractive features. Her face seemed to be lined by kindness and this kindness shone more brightly when she smiled. "I went to the dog races," he explained while he walked beside her toward the camp. "I bet on Hunter and won. I also made bets for you and Will." Giving her the two packets, he said, "These are your winnings. One is for you. The other is for Will."

"Thank you," she said, accepting the packages. "Good things come our way. You've done well. Don't get thinking you'll win again though. You've been lucky once. No one wins often at gambling. Hunter's a good dog. I want him to race a few more times before he retires. Will wants Hunter to retire now so when Will went back to see his family in the Smoky Mountains, he took the dog with him." Starting to walk along the trail, she added, "Come and get some food."

Seth followed Sihoki to her cooking fire where he was again served stew along with coffee. He was sipping coffee contentedly when Sihoki smoothed an area of sand near the bench. Using a stick, she drew a map in this sand. As the end of the stick outlined a small circle in the sand, she explained, "We are here." Moving the stick again to make a line heading northward, she said,

Pelican Moon

"My brother took Hunter north to the Smokies. You take these roads to this trail and you will find my brother."

"I'm going to go there?" he asked, incredulously.

"Yes," she replied.

"Do you think I'll get there?" asked Seth doubting that he could remember the map.

Drawing the stick through the sand, repeating the route, Sihoki said, "You just drive north to this trail. Follow it and you will find a village in the mountains." After the stick had scratched another circle, she said, "Will is here." Giving Seth a packet of money, she continued to say, "On your way north, please give Will this money you won for him at the track. Also ask him to return Hog Hunter for a last series of races. Then Hunter can retire."

"Okay, I'll try," replied Seth.

"You'll find Will's mountain camp," affirmed Sihoki. "Hog Hunter will come back to finish his races."

"How can you be so sure of things?" asked Seth with growing respect for the woman's abilities.

"The spirit world only seems mysterious to those who don't seek or look," she answered. "The future can be as well known as the past. In the spirit, one can travel back and forth. We can let things happen as they happen or we can make plans. I prefer a planned life to a random existence."

"There's a lot o' things I don't understand," admitted Seth. "Thank you for your advice, including stew and coffee. I'll find your brother for you. Such a journey is going to be interesting."

"You have an interesting journey ahead of you, back and forth," she replied with her eyes sparkling.

By the look on her face, Seth knew she could say much more although she chose not to. She did not say more and Seth didn't ask. To himself, he said, if I'm to know something, I'll find out soon enough.

"You can't escape these things," countered Sihoki as if she had read his thoughts.

"I'll see things when I get to them," said Seth, more to himself than to Sihoki. "I don't mind taking one day at a time. I don't have to see into the distance."

"The future is more important than the past," countered Sihoki.

"Doesn't one's past effect one's future?" he asked. He was getting tired of all her talk about things he could not see.

"Yes," she answered. "But where we are headed is more important than where we've been."

"What do you see in my future?" asked Seth wanting to get to something more definite.

"I've often wondered why we are not told more," replied Sihoki as she looked out toward the swamp. "I think we are only told as much as we will believe. That's why we only see a small piece of our lives at one time. When we leave this physical state and return to the spirit world, we understand everything and the whole experience makes sense. What I tell you now won't change anything."

Finishing the coffee, Seth placed his empty cup on the table, saying, "Thanks again. That's good coffee." He stood up and said, "I'll find your brother in the Smoky Mountains. I'll give him this money and ask him to bring Hog Hunter back here for some final races."

"When Hog Hunter returns," said Sihoki with her usual confidence, "bet on him. Thanks for sharing your winnings the first time; however, you don't have to do that again. Don't think you'll always win at gambling because people generally lose."

Sihoki walked with Seth to the river. He pushed his canoe into the water then stepped into the craft using balance acquired through innumerable experiences. After sitting down, he dipped the paddle into cool, clear water. Turning the craft upstream, he said, "Thanks for your help. I'll be seeing you."

"Come back soon," she replied. She waved to him just before he moved out of view beyond verdant foliage.

I have only known Sihoki and Will briefly, reflected Sethrum. However, they have become my friends and I feel I have known them for a long time. I am also intrigued by the way I seem to have been drawn into a plan that was not of my own making. How many people can really say they mapped out their lives and then followed this plan? I'm now heading north to find Will Panther because I initially went shark fishing. Sihoki Panther possibly knows more about my future than I do.

Seth paddled upstream until, on the shore, he recognized the familiar outline of his truck. After tieing his canoe onto the truck, he drove northward and started a long journey, mapped in sand as well as spirit.

FOUR

FLOP EAR

Sethrum Moon traveled north, following a route marked on a map which lingered in his memory from a sketch drawn in sand by Sihoki. He completed the first part of the map by taking main highways leading north. Gradually, in the distance, mountains appeared. They were partially veiled by a blue haze.

Upon reaching mountainous country, a mixture of paved and graveled roads took the place of a remembered path in sand. This route kept climbing to an higher elevation in a way that avoided towns or cities. In a secluded area, Sethrum pitched his tent beside a swiftly flowing stream. Northward, clouds obscured mountain peaks. To the south, lesser mountains and rolling hills receded into a blue mist.

Seth smoked a cigar while he rested and watched hills that unfolded into the distance southward. Red bud trees along with dogwoods added a scattering of mauve and white colors to verdant slopes. Two turkey vultures soared over the treetops. At a greater height, an eagle's broad wings were etched in pink light from the setting sun. This light matched the red, clay earth in a green landscape sprinkled with wild flowers and blossoms.

During this trip, reflected Sethrum, I've seen a few deer in addition to some turkeys strutting on an hilltop. There are bears around here along with rattlesnakes, wild hogs and panthers. The Florida panther is apparently somewhat different from northern panthers. These northern cats are also called pumas, cougars or mountain lions. Traveling by myself, I'm mainly concerned about bears, although people are the most dangerous things in the woods. Sihoki seemed to think I'm on some kind of a spiritual journey. I started out on a shark-fishing trip and now I find myself on a spiritual journey outlined to me by Sihoki. I think she gets most of her information from visions. Maybe we are all on spiritual journeys and they are so connected there's no such thing as a coincidence.

Seth unpacked a few shark fillets he had stored on ice. He first shook them in a bag containing flour before frying them in particularly hot oil. When the fillets had turned a dark, golden color, they were placed on a paper plate. He sprinkled salt and pepper, in addition to vinegar, on the steaming, fragrant fillets then used a plastic knife and fork to cut the white, moist meat. I can burn these utensils after I've finished with them, he said to himself as he savored the flaky, tender fish.

I'll go to any length to avoid washing dishes.

Following the meal, Seth put a few extra fillets on a rock jutting into the water downstream. By the time he returned to his camp, a red sunset was being reflected on the stream turning it to a ribbon of crimson light winding through the forest. This pathway faded until it later caught a silver sheen from the moon. Seth added wood to his fire, feeding a steady blaze. Through openings in a canopy of branches, Seth watched the starlit sky with its rising moon.

He slept beside his fire until he was awakened by the sounds of snapping twigs. Twigs, along with a few larger branches, cracked sharply in regular intervals as if a person was walking steadily through the forest. The campfire had diminished to a few remnant embers. Only the moon gave light to the woods. Snapping sounds became louder as the thing came closer to the camp.

Someone or something is walking directly toward me, Sethrum warned himself.

Remaining still, Seth watched his surroundings carefully although he couldn't see anything moving among the shadows. Something big is out there because it has been breaking large sticks or branches, observed Seth as his discomfort increased. I'm in a strange place. Shadows lurk everywhere and there could be anything out there. I'm now fully awake. I'll get my flashlight and check my rifle.

Seth switched on his flashlight and had his rifle ready for firing. He thought he heard branches rustling near camp. That gurgling sound of the stream would hide a lot of other noises, he said to himself. I got careless, I guess. I usually don't camp in such places.

Shocked to realize he had not seen the thing earlier, he suddenly noticed some of the shadows had taken the distinct shape of a large bear. The creature stood up among pine trunks and watched the river. Dropping agilely to all four paws, the bear turned and started walking directly toward camp. That giant probably doesn't know I'm here, Seth told himself. It might stumble right into my camp. I don't want to have to confront a surprised bear at close range. He's getting too close. Seth stood up, waved his arms and shouted, "Go on! Get out o' here!"

The bear was so surprised by the shouting that the animal seemed to trip. Regaining some composure, the bear stood on hind legs and looked at the camp. The animal hesitated and appeared to be uncertain as to what to do.

Wheeling around with surprising speed, the large creature ran to the creek, crossed it and became lost from view among a tangle of shadows and trees. Later, a splashing sound, distinctly different from the steady murmur of the water, came from downstream near the outcropping of rock.

Pelican Moon

After the bear's departure, Sethrum rebuilt his fire, toasted some bread then fried bacon followed by eggs. In dawn's gray light, he was dipping water from the stream when he saw a small snake on a muddy section of the bank. A shadow crossed the bank as an heron glided overhead. A whirring sound of wings brought Seth's attention to two ducks flying across the sky. Flying side by side, they quickly moved out of sight. The forest is full of life, noted Sethrum, particularly in the spring or early summer.

He filled the coffeepot with water in addition to aromatic, ground coffee and placed this pot at the fire's edge. Looking around at the woods, he thought, the forest is endlessly interesting. Since there's too much to see at any one time, I enjoy sitting in an high area and watching the wilderness with all its life and moods. Wild places have immeasurable beauty. Many people are aware of such beauty; yet they also think of these places as being just wastelands to be exploited or otherwise destroyed. The present use of tree farms makes logging in a wilderness unnecessary. The growing of hemp would also provide a preferred substitute for wood in many cases. People shouldn't lose a forest just because a logging company doesn't want to plan ahead and plant the company's own trees. Destructive logging, such as clear-cutting of trees should never be allowed in a forest. Business people today have learned that a living forest brings in more money than can be obtained through logging. When loggers kill a forest, they even put themselves out of business.

Seth was distracted from his thoughts by the sight of a vulture flying up from the rock downstream where the fish had been placed. Turkey vultures certainly do look like turkeys, observed Seth while the bird flew to the branch of a dead pine. A gray fox had taken the vulture's place at the rock. I enjoy the companionship of life in a forest, reflected Seth. I'm amazed by how much the forest's critters have in common with people. Bear hunters say the best food for baiting bears is donuts.

Sethrum was refilling his coffee cup when he heard a plaintive howl of a wolf. Following a brief silence, a train's whistle could be heard accompanied by a distant rumble. This sound faded gradually to be replaced by silence. A passing train often causes wolves to howl, thought Seth. Maybe the howl came from a red wolf. I'm pleased that people are helping red wolves come back to the Smokies. Farmers could receive compensation from the government, as a type of insurance policy, to make up for any loss of stock. I particularly like wolves because they don't bother people. Bears, cougars and rattlesnakes are dangerous although they too have a place in the wild. A wolf's howl is a necessary part of a real wilderness.

Coming from the vicinity of the rock outcropping, Seth heard a splashing sound that could clearly be distinguished from the background murmuring of the river. Shortly afterward, a dog barked. The barking continued and kept getting louder.

Looking toward the rock, Seth saw a wild hog sniffing at the fish. There can't be many hogs around here, Seth said to himself while reaching for his rifle.

Aiming his rifle at the boar, Seth thought, I seem to have located a particularly wild area here. The boar looked up toward the far bank where there was a crouched form of a cougar.

There can't be many cougars around these parts, Seth said to himself just before the large cat sprang off the bank. Issuing a startled grunt, the pig lurched sideways, causing the cat to claw only air then hit shallow water and an edge of the rock. The boar charged upstream toward Seth's camp and waiting rifle.

Before Seth could fire, a shadowy form of a greyhound attacked from the side, hitting the hog in a plume of spray. Both animals, with legs kicking, tumbled into the water. The hog broke away and ran downstream only to be blocked and sent back by the cougar. Both dog and cat attacked and the hog defended itself furiously. A powerful blow from the cat's paw sent the boar tumbling into a sprawling roll. The animal regained its feet and tried to retreat by running toward Seth. Seeing the dog and cougar come out of the water on the south side, Seth took his one chance for a shot and aimed beneath the charging, squealing head. The rifle blasted at the running form, knocking it down into a leg-kicking roll. The greyhound attacked from the side then the cougar got a neck hold and shook furiously, finishing the battle.

The greyhound left the boar and ran at Seth with such speed the leaping movements were blurred. Seth was gripped by shock. That must be Hog Hunter but what if it isn't, thought Seth before he was knocked over in a rush that ended in a tumultuous greeting. Relief washed over Seth as he stayed on his back, looked up and ran his hands along the dog's head. "If you hadn't been Hog Hunter, I wouldn't have had a chance to defend myself," said Seth to Hunter before the dog turned and walked toward the cougar. The large cat, glancing warily at Seth, moved out of view beyond foliage. Hunter travels with a cougar, Seth told himself. Sihoki said Hunter sometimes hunted with a panther in the swamp. Both hunters help each other to catch hogs. Friends are made during good as well as bad times.

Sethrum butchered the hog. After completing the work, he placed the leftover portions on the rock downstream. Next he skewered a chunk of pork over the fire. Hunter rested in camp and eagerly watched the roasting meat. The cougar ate meat at the rock outcropping. The cat is an old, battle-scarred female, noted Seth. She probably needs or at least likes help to hunt. With one ear flopped down, along with other scarred irregularities, the old cat looks like she had been put together by an incompetent taxidermist. I'll call her Flop Ear.

Having cooked the meat, Seth cut it into three large pieces, giving the first piece to Hog Hunter. His jaws quivered as they gripped the warm, oily meat. He stretched out on the ground, tucked the food between his front paws, and ate contentedly. The second chunk was thrown to some bushes where the cat had been resting. Saving the smallest piece, Seth sprinkled it with salt as well as pepper then cut off a slab and chewed it slowly, savoring this tender, flavorful meat. Seth had also perked coffee. It was sipped during the meal of roasted pork. To the dog, Seth said, "Since you are here, I must've followed directions correctly and I'll soon find Will Panther. One of the lines Sihoki scratched in sand represents this river, or a path along the riverbank. You will help me find Will Panther."

FIVE

<u>THE TRAIL</u>

Sethrum's camp was comfortable. The campers were an odd trio. Seth enjoyed watching the dog and cougar working together as they checked scents and trails. Both hunters seemed accustomed to traveling with each other. That old cat has probably taught Hunter a lot about hunting, thought Sethrum after the dog and cougar had left camp to check a new scent. I can't get close to the cougar, although she tolerates me because I'm obviously Hunter's friend. The cat is more inclined to locate one, promising scent and stay with it, whereas the dog wanders more from one track to another. I'm convinced this river marks the route to the mountains that Sihoki etched in sand. If I could get Flop Ear to stay on this route, I would have a guide to follow if the trail wanders very far from the riverbank. So far, I haven't found an actual path although there must be one.

In the gray light provided by the following dawn, Sethrum left his camp and truck behind. He carried two packs, along with his rifle, and started walking beside the water. He headed upstream, to the north. Of the three travelers, the cougar went first. Next came Hog Hunter. He kept running back to check on Seth before dashing ahead again.

The cat is traveling in the right direction for me, reasoned Seth. She's following a game trail although people also use the same path. I suppose most human paths were originally game trails. Sihoki marked in sand the same route being taken now by Flop Ear.

Pelican Moon

When the cat turned away from the river, Seth suspected that the old hunter had left the main path. The water is to the south, noted Seth. I can easily go back. First I'll see why Flop Ear changed directions.

The upward climb was tiring and Seth had to stop occasionally. While resting, he watched clouds drifting passed mountaintops in a landscape colored by a blue tint of an haze that deepened along the horizon. On the mountainside, deer tracks mingled with the occasional prints of bears and wild turkeys. When Hog Hunter caught a wild turkey, Seth prepared a camp. He used a spit to cook the bird over a steadily flickering flame provided by dry, oak firewood. The meat contained little fat, yet cooked well and supplied a meal for the three travelers.

Seth made coffee and sipped the drink slowly while he considered his situation. I'm on a strange journey, he told himself. I started by going shark fishing and have ended up following a map I can vaguely remember because it existed briefly in sand. The woman who gave me this map said I'm on a journey that very few other people experience. My present companions are a flop-eared cougar and a greyhound. I think the cougar has led me away from the trail I want to follow. The river borders my route. I would, however, like to see where the cougar is going. I have a rare opportunity to follow a mountain lion. There's probably an old den up here somewhere.

The next morning, when the cougar got restless and left the campsite, Seth was ready to follow. Upward, always upward, the cat traveled until it reached a plateau. On the more level area, Seth prepared another camping place.

From beyond clouds hiding the mountaintop, an eagle screamed. Ravens called raucously. They appeared briefly as they flew through mist. Their broad wings could be heard brushing against

Pelican Moon

moist air. "Flop Ear leaves us most of the time now," said Seth to Hunter. The dog was watching pork being roasted over the fire. "That cat is at home here."

When picking up dead branches for firewood, Seth noticed an unusually intricate pattern on one branch just as he was reaching for it. He jumped back and shook, realizing he had almost picked up a large rattlesnake. The disturbed reptile buzzed loudly before coiling. Seth held a long stick in front of the reptile and the stick was struck with surprising force. Moving too quickly to be blocked, Hog Hunter sprang forward, grabbed a back section of the creature and shook it wildly, killing the snake almost instantly. Later in the day, amid the shadows of evening, the cougar returned and got a meal of roasted pork.

The next day, vapor drifting through camp created a ghostly atmosphere obscuring most things except the flickering fire and persistent sounds of scratching or digging. Walking toward the source of these clawing noises, Seth saw Hog Hunter. The dog was digging frantically as if being near the scent of an animal. Looking more closely, Seth realized that Hunter was enlarging an hole left in the ground where a rock had previously been removed to be placed around the campfire. Hunter had clawed out smaller stones, making a large opening.

When Sethrum checked the hole, a current of upward flowing cool air brushed against his face. "What kind o' strange thing have you uncovered?" Seth asked Hunter just before the dog lost his grip at the edge of the pit and fell inside. Seth frantically tried to grab the dog but grasped only air. The dog had descended into darkness. An horrifying silence was followed by a muted thud then sharp barking came from inside the ground.

Stunned by what had happened, Seth stared at he opening in disbelief. Fear stuck in his throat, making his mouth dry while his heart beat faster. He was sweating. "How am I going to get that dog out o' there?" he whispered to the surrounding shadows. All I can do is get my rope and flashlight, he decided.

He ran to camp, got a rope and flashlight then rushed back to the gaping darkness of the opening. What a mess to get into, he said to himself as he shone the light into a deep, rock-sided tunnel. He called to Hunter and was answered by distant barking.

I don't think he's injured, thought Seth after he tied one end of the rope to a tree. Carrying the rest of the rope to the hole, he thought, Hunter can bark. If he was injured, he would be yelping or whining.

Having dropped the loose end of the rope into the gap, Seth double-checked the other end. He was certain his knot would hold. With flashlight under one arm, he tightly held the rope and eased himself into the tunnel. He gripped the rope while pushing his back and legs against vertical, rock sides. He kept the light turned on in an attempt to see what kind of a cavern he was entering. When his boots touched a rock floor, he searched with the light, yet could not see Hog Hunter. Only a dog would wander off at a time like this, Seth said to himself in frustration. He stared in awe along the beam of light. It outlined a cavern containing ghostly, stone configurations. Colossal spears of stalagmites were aimed upward from the floor. Resembling grotesque icicles, stalactites hung down from a ceiling bordered by walls of stone columns along with wider, curtain-like formations.

Walking forward slowly, keeping attached to the rope, he entered a massive chamber which was much like an earthen cathedral partially filled by a formation resembling a waterfall that had been instantly turned to rock. Water dripping from stalactites pock marked a pool and moved ripples under a reflection of the surrounding chamber.

When he ran out of rope, Seth used his knife to scratch a trail to another chasm. A cougar's snarl filled this cavern, sending a chill through Seth. Seeing something move beside him, he turned in time to have two paws slam against his chest in a greeting from Hog Hunter. The dog whined while resting his head against the side of Seth's shoulder. An outline of the cougar appeared in dim light ahead. "Good to see you're all right," said Seth to Hunter before the dog dropped down to the rocky floor and started walking toward the cougar. We have to get out of here, Seth told himself. The cat probably lives in these caverns. Maybe we can get out the way the cat got in.

Continuing to scratch out a trail, Sethrum followed Hunter toward the form of the cougar outlined in pale light. With a fury that seemed like an explosion of action in the confines of the cavern, Hunter started shaking something. The cougar's snarl was loud and piercing. Caught in the light's beam, there appeared a long, limp form of a black snake hanging from Hunter's jaws. Near the dog's feet, an human skull protruded from sand.

Hunter led Seth to an horizontal opening large enough for a person to crawl through. Cougar fur matted the floor of this break. Seth crawled into this opening and stepped into moonlight. He was on the face of a cliff where mist drifted in surrealistic light from the moon. A trail on a ledge wound away from a narrow cave. Gurgling sounds from the river below clearly pierced the solitude. At least I know where I am now, Seth thought. I'm back at the river although I don't like that narrow ledge. It's very eroded and seems to lead into nothing but air. Only a cougar could use it now. People used it, maybe even made much of it a long time ago. Human travelers today follow the banks of the river. I'll have to get out of here the same way I came in.

While the cat remained near the opening, Hunter followed Seth to the rope hanging from a break in ceiling rocks. Hunter didn't resist being tied over Seth's shoulders. The dog seemed to understand something of the situation and any lack in comprehension was covered by trust.

The added weight of having Hunter on Seth's shoulders made the climb up the rope an agonizing ordeal. Again Seth pushed his legs and back against the stone walls to take the strain off his hold on the rope. Both man and dog were relieved to escape from the earth. Seth resealed the tunnel by covering it with slabs of rock. He was trembling with weariness when he returned to his camp. The fire had dwindled to embers. Without taking time to rebuild the fire he stretched out on the ground and rested while watching the sky. He saw two shooting stars blaze a bright path across the starlit expanse then he slept soundly.

In the morning, Seth packed his equipment and walked to the river. He enjoyed washing in cold water. It also revived sore muscles. Near the water, he discovered a path bordering the bank. He followed Hunter along this trail. It constantly wound upward toward a mountaintop forested largely by oaks and hemlocks. Toward the middle of the day, the cougar rejoined the group.

In the afternoon, the tired travelers stopped at a long, narrow cave. Its ceiling rocks had been blackened by smoke from a fire pit located in the center of the shallow room. The dog and cougar immediately explored the farthest edges of the interior. Hunter growled deeply before grabbing and shaking a large rattlesnake. "We should call you Snake Hunter," said Seth to the dog. When the ropelike form of the snake was dropped onto the floor of the cave, Seth slid a stick under the limp creature and swung it into the forest.

Inside the shelter, beside a back ledge, bones protruded from sandy clay. They appeared to be from caribou as well as musk ox. People have been using these caves for a long time, noted Sethrum. Maybe people didn't use the cavern much except for one person who possibly got lost in there.

Along interior walls, torches were wedged between horizontal slabs of rock. Seth lit one torch. A twisting flame snapped sharply while sending a tendril of smoke up to the ceiling. This bluish line of smoke gradually curled out of the chamber. Light jumped across stone walls, revealing drawings resembling elk along with buffalo. Pieces of pottery were partially buried beside the fire pit. More pieces were scattered at the base of the walls. Cougars lived below in the caverns, observed Seth, while human hunters used this cave. Ancient people hunted caribou and musk ox.

Later groups were after elk in addition to buffalo. More recently, Cherokee hunters probably stayed here. They'd be hunting deer and bear.

When Sethrum stepped outside the cave, strands of drifting vapor obscured much of the lower landscape. I'm actually above the clouds, he said to himself. Far overhead, sunlight emblazoned the wings of two soaring eagles.

Hunter and Flop Ear rested beside the shelter while Seth started a small fire on top of the fire pit. Sunlight tinted the area with a golden sheen. Vapors stretched themselves in sunlight, always moving.

Broad wings brushed against moist air, bringing a vulture to get the dead rattlesnake. Carrying this reptile, the large, black bird flew toward gnarled branches of a dead oak. My visit to these mountains, thought Seth, is like a journey through time because little has changed. I can appreciate this wilderness as others before me have seen it. Old Flop ear might be the last cougar of her time. There is an incalculable loss when life is allowed to pass or leave. These mountains almost lost the legend of the Cherokees. Sihoki said God gives spiritual insights to us through visions of the past, present and future. She said I would receive a vision whether I sought one or not.

With the addition of more dry, oak branches to the fire, a tall, crackling flame sent light dancing across the cave's entrance. Seth filled his coffeepot from a small, spring-fed pool he located near the trail. He prepared coffee, poured a cupful then sipped the flavorful drink while he observed mountainsides topped with oaks mixed with majestic hemlocks. Mountain laurel also added green luster to slopes. Forested ridges undulated through a blue veil that darkened with distance. Ravens called raucously as they frolicked in flight. Two vultures soared above the ravens. Beyond the vultures, there will be an eagle somewhere, mused Seth.

The bluish landscape received pink shafts of light from a mauve horizon where the sun was setting. Gradually this burst of light withdrew, leaving behind a darkening forest.

Seth roasted pork over tall flames that cooked the meat quickly. Hog Hunter's tail wagged when he saw the meat being removed from a spit. The dog, cat and man each received a large share for a fine meal. Afterward, Seth poured more coffee and watched flames brighten a small area of the night. A wolf howled from a neighboring mountainside. Howls echoed among slopes being brushed by clouds. Later, moonlight shone upon a wild land.

Sethrum woke up amid growls and snarls coming from the back of the cave. The following silence was broken only by scuffling sounds then Hunter walked to the entranceway. From his jaws, dangled a torn rattlesnake. When Hunter dropped the long, limp form, Seth shoved a stick under it and tossed it toward murky shapes of trees below camp.

Like his two companions, Seth slept intermittently. Each time he woke up, he added wood to the fire. We waste a lot of beautiful time sleeping, he thought before he saw a bear with two cups cross a moonlit clearing on a lower slope.

At daybreak, the cougar carried a turkey into camp. Seth cooked this meat. It provided a large breakfast. The cat had quickly become accustomed to cooked meat.

Following a breakfast of roasted turkey, the cougar, dog and man left their camp and walked down through a damp forest. The air was cold as well as humid.

Sethrum returned to the river and followed this landmark to a place where it was joined by a tributary. Seth rested here and built a fire to prepare green tea. With the dog, he shared some roasted meat. That cougar has been missing for a long time, observed Seth. I think I have traveled too far away from the cat's home area and the old cougar has likely returned to the cavern. By heading north, I think I lost the main path. This second stream is a tributary and maybe it will lead me to the village. If this route leads nowhere, I'm lost. I'm not a quitter; but I want to reach the camp soon or I'll go back.

He decided to camp for the night beside the new stream. He roasted the last of his supply of pork, sending tantalizing aromas drifting with air currents stirring restlessly among the mountains. An eagle's cry penetrated a thick haze where ravens called and two vultures soared. An oak-edged skyline dimmed with deepening blue tints of evening.

While resting and sipping tea, Seth remembered that Hunter had wandered back up the slope and had not returned. Maybe Hunter has gone back to visit Flop Ear, thought Seth. I think the old cat lives near, or in, the caverns. She probably finds hunting to be increasingly difficult so she likes Hunter's help. She probably enjoys the dog's company just like I do. If the cougar lives in the cavern and doesn't wander away, she must have met Hunter around here. Hunter would have come from Will Panther's village and this village must be nearby. There has to be a better way to get to the village.

A snapping twig distracted Seth. Looking into a tangle of shadows surrounding him, he saw one deer and then others. Like stirring shadows, they bounded out of view just before Hunter returned to stretch out wearily near the fire.

I like these mountains, reflected Seth, pleased that the dog had returned.

There's a wild spirit in these hills. The dog and I are part of that spirit. In its presence, I feel I'm at home. The beauty of these mountains has seeped into my soul, giving me an appreciation for lofty places. Each type of landscape has unique beauty. I also enjoy the Gulf Coast of Florida.

Clouds moved away from the moon. It dropped a silver sheen into the night, creating a more intricate array of shadows. Red wolves howled before the moon was hidden again. Seth slept soundly until he woke up in the gray light of dawn. Cold, moist air added a sharp edge to a breeze that stirred restlessly among verdant slopes. Without waiting to make coffee, Seth left his camp. He thought he had to travel anyway so he could get warm by walking rather than by taking time to build a fire. He followed Hog Hunter along a well-marked path. It crossed from the far side of the river and wound westward.

Hog Hunter usually ran ahead and had to keep rushing back to check Seth's progress. This routine of traveling brought the companions to the start of a series of rapids. From here, the trail turned northward into increasingly high terrain. Hunger and weariness gnawed at Seth until he decided to make camp. Flames from his campfire brightened against a background of darkening shadows. After the last remnants of sunlight had left the mountaintops, evening murkiness settled quickly around camp. Seth and Hunter slept while fog moved among trees and drifted passed the fire. Its flames diminished until only embers greeted the dawn.

First rays of morning sunlight shot passed oak-crested ridges and sprayed the air with wedges of gold. One section of this light caught a dog then a man during their walk along a well-used trail. A tributary of the river fell along a rock face, tumbling in tendrils of spray that caused a whispering sound before gathering into a stream near the path.

Seth enjoyed each new scene around every bend; but he was shaken when he first saw the ledge. It crossed a rock face dropping into a gorge. From the base of this gorge, Seth could hear the sounds of rushing water that must be rapids in the main river. I don't like sheer drops, Seth told himself while he felt his nerves tighten.

Ravens croaked while flying through misty, blue-tinted air. With worry quickly becoming unnerving fear, Seth stepped out onto the ledge. I like solid, firm places more than steep cliffs, he thought as his hands searched for gripping places among cold, damp ridges on the rock wall. On the opposite side, curling mist moved together with hissing sounds of falling water. He progressed slowly in what seemed to be a walk across the sky. His heart pounded and throat became dry. Seeing the end of the cliff appear, he walked more quickly and was greatly relieved when his boots hit solid ground away from the ledge.

Leaving the gorge out of sight behind him, Sethrum sat down and used a match to coax smoke from a crumpled cigar. Relaxing completely, he watched tendrils of bluish smoke curl upward beside an hemlock stump silhouetted against clouds drifting above a tapestry of slopes. Hearing a shrill, quivering cry of an eagle, Seth caught a glimpse of the soaring bird before it became lost in a sunlit haze.

Upon finishing the cigar, Seth continued walking. He pushed onward until he could detect in the air a distinct fragrance of wood smoke. This scent increased when he reached a clearing surrounded by oaks on a rounded top of the mountain. Buildings were made of logs and had stone chimneys. A young girl and woman both greeted Hog Hunter. Seth asked the woman, "Where is Will Panther's house?"

"Over there," answered the woman who pointed to the farthest cabin facing north, overlooking the sky. "The dog will show you."

"Thanks," replied Seth. "I should have thought about Hunter knowing the way. He's heading for the house."

When Seth approached the cabin, a person opened the door and Hunter entered the building. Keeping the door open, Will Panther said, "I see Hunter has brought us Sethrum Moon."

SIX

WILL PANTHER

Sethrum was welcomed into a log home containing a kitchen, bedrooms and bathroom connected to a central room where a chesterfield along with chairs faced a fireplace containing a tall, steady flame. Opposite this fireplace, a large window, on the north wall, provided a view of sky above mountain peaks. In a distant, blue valley, roofs of a few buildings shone in sunlight.

"There's an eagle," said Will as he pointed to a broad winged bird gliding through golden tints above peaks. Turning toward Seth, noting his equipment, Will added, "You can leave your stuff in the closet beside the door. I guess Sihoki sent you or you'd never have found this place."

"Yes, she did," answered Seth after he placed his traveling packs on the closet's floor.

"We don't get many visitors here," continued Will. "Are you hungry?"

"No, thanks," he replied.

"Sit down beside the fire," said Will. "I'll get coffee." Will walked to the kitchen, poured coffee then served Seth a cup of the steaming, fragrant drink. He placed a second cup of coffee on a table beside an adjacent chair. "I'm going to put fresh water in Hog Hunter's bucket," explained Will. "I'll be right back."

Will filled Hunter's bucket and the dog drank noisily before stretching out on the floor in front of the fireplace. Will returned to his chair, sipped coffee and said, "This is my wife's house. She's away visiting our daughter. We have three daughters, one son and five grandchildren."

While listening to Will talking with background sounds of flames snapping in the fireplace, Seth thought, Will is knowledgeable about most things. He can work at a variety of jobs. He's a experienced and interesting person who is very easy to talk to.

Outside the window, clouds drifted across hemlocks. One particularly gnarled stump was silhouetted against a backdrop of drifting vapor. Inside the cabin, the fire snapped while providing heat along with flickering light. After refilling both cups with more coffee, Will said, "I get orders from my wife all the time. Now I suppose I'm about to get one from my sister. If there's anything my wife forgets to tell me to do, my sister thinks of it."

"You're right about your sister," said Seth. "I guess Sihoki is good at telling me what to do also. She asked me to come here and give you a message. She wants you to let Hog Hunter run in a last series of races before he retires.

She says he has these races in him and he should run them. She knows he's more of a friend to you than a racer so you want to take him out of the business. Sihoki thinks the dog should go to his limits. He's a champion and kindness is letting him run as long as possible, meaning one last series of races."

"The dog can certainly take one last series," agreed Will. "I just didn't want him to overstay his time. Speaking of time, do you have time to take him back?"

"Yes, I could do that," answered Seth.

"Thanks," said Will, looking relieved.

"Is this an old village?" asked Seth.

"This village," replied Will as he looked out the window, seeming to be looking into the past where his thoughts had taken him, "has been here as long as the Cherokees have been in these mountains. My ancestors are Tocobaga and Creek. They became called

Pelican Moon

Seminoles. My wife is Cherokee. The Cherokee nation is one of the Iroquoian nations. They once lived near the mouth of the Mississippi River and were neighbors of the Wolf, or Pawnee, nation. I have heard that the Pawnee and Iroquoian languages are similar. The Iroquoians traveled up the Mississippi River and, at the Great Lakes, divided into groups that, through time, became different nations. The Haudenosaunee, or People of the Longhouse, formed the League of Five—later the League of Six—Nations, made up of the Mohawk, Oneida, Onondaga, Cayuga, Seneca and Tuscarora. Meanwhile, the Cherokee had traveled southward and settled in a large area including these mountains."

With added sparkle in his eyes, Will continued to say, "Our homeland has been whittled away by all types of people. The worst of them were the politicians who would have taken away all our land and given it to anyone else. President

Jackson and others tried to remove us along the Trail of Tears to Oklahoma during 1838 and 1839. Against all these odds, some of the Cherokee stayed to give their contributions toward making America the great nation it is today."

After drinking coffee, Will said, "long ago, Indian hunters could go to the land any time, almost anywhere, and get food from nature's resources. Today, the wilderness is smaller and we must more closely regulate hunting and fishing or too much will be taken and everyone will lose. We need more common sense in all things. I guess common sense would allow Hog Hunter to finish a last series of races before he retires."

"Yes," agreed Sethrum, "that sounds fair. A fair solution would solve anything."

For himself and Seth along with Hunter, Will served slices of pork that he had barbecued on a spit in the fireplace. Next, he poured draft beer into tall glasses. Keeping one glass for himself, he brought the other to Seth.

"Thanks," Said Seth. "These are great treats, particularly after a long walk."

Pointing to screened openings below the windows, Will explained, "I installed ventilators to provide air for the fireplace and to remove smoke. I enjoy a fireplace and like to smoke a pipe although I don't like having smoke in a room."

"Thanks for your hospitality," said Sethrum before he stood up to take his empty glass to the kitchen sink. "Maybe I should get started if I'm going to take Hunter to Sihoki. She says I'm headed for some kind of a spiritual journey."

"She knows about things like that," said Will. "She also has a knowledge of natural medicines. A university is researching her remedies."

"She's almost too knowledgeable," said Seth. "I'll have to be careful about what I tell her."

"You do that," affirmed Will as a smile crossed his face.

"I'll return Hog Hunter then I must go north and get back to work," said Seth. "I started out by going shark fishing and ended up with a dog and have met a woman who tells me I'm on a different kind of journey. Do you know that Hunter sometimes travels with a cougar?"

"That dog's a runner and a traveler," said Will. "He also likes company so he will travel with a cougar. The dog isn't a real killer. If a bird injures itself by flying against a window, Hunter will bring that bird inside without hurting it. I think he only hunts hogs, snakes and a few turkeys. I've seen him with an old cougar east of here and he sometimes travels with a panther in Florida."

"You've seen the caverns?" asked Seth as he went to get his packs in the closet. He placed them over his shoulder.

"Yes," answered Will. He followed Seth to the doorway. Hunter was the first one to reach the door. He was eager to be going on the walk that seemed to be coming. "The cougar lives in the front part of the caverns," continued Will. "Sometimes when I go to the upper cave with Hunter, the cougar follows us."

Sethrum stepped outside with Will and Hunter. Drifting clouds obscured much of the landscape. "I'll probably retire soon from training dogs because I'd sooner keep them just as pets," said Will.

"That's probably why your dogs are such good racers," observed Seth.

When Hunter finishes his races, maybe he, the cougar and I will retire to these mountains," said Will. "After being to the high places, I have difficulty finding contentment anywhere else, although I like the everglades."

"I almost forgot," exclaimed Sethrum, reaching into his jacket pocket. "I placed a trifecta bet on Hunter for you. You won this money."

Will, accepting the cash, said softly, "It's always a pleasure to meet an honest person—and a winner too. This is almost more than I can believe. I know Hunter can be a winner; but I've never won at betting and you'll lose too if you keep gambling. Thank you very much anyway. This is more than I could expect."

"I placed the same bet for Sihoki," added Seth. "She won the same amount."

Returning some money to Sethrum, Will said, "Maybe your luck will extend to another race. But don't keep betting. Use this money to place bets for you, Sihoki and me. I know Hunter is in top form. I mainly brought him here for company because otherwise I would have been alone on the trip. I guess Sihoki thought I was trying to get him completely out of racing—and she's right. As my sister probably told you, Hunter isn't the fastest dog; yet he has heart and likes wet conditions. He loves water. Depending on the other dogs, as well as conditions, Hunter could easily beat the odds and come in first. If he came in first, the winnings would be large. Remember, though, a person shouldn't bet with the expectation of winning. However, Sihoki and I know this dog. People at the track have been writing him off before his time. Sihoki thought that maybe I was doing the same thing. Right now, Hunter's as good, or better, than he ever was. He's accustomed to cold weather because of these mountains. He loves water on account o' the everglades. During rough weather that he likes, a dog with heart will win against the odds."

Having placed the money in a pocket inside his jacket, Seth said, "I'll place the bets for you and thanks for everything." Seth adjusted his packs. Hunter had started walking eastward. "I've so much to do," continued Seth, "I'd better get started."

"If we've done our best, we have nothing to worry about," said Will. "Thanks for sharing your winnings."

"I'll take care o' your mutt," said Seth before he turned and started walking into drifting mist.

"That's some mutt," replied Will. Mist obscured Seth who followed Hunter toward the east.

When Seth met Hunter at the edge of the village, breaks in clouds revealed a raven soaring above treetops on the mountainside. Hunter dashed forward again, rushing along the path. Remnant tendrils of vapor drifted away from a vast vista of undulating blue slopes.

Toward evening, Seth prepared a camp on a site that was sheltered by rocks as well as trees and the area had abundant firewood. While enjoying the warmth of

Pelican Moon

a flickering, snapping fire, Sethrum thought, all I planned to do was to go shark fishing. Instead of catching a shark, the shark seemed to catch me and started me on a journey. So far, I've met great people along with a dog. This land has spectacular beauty. There is wilderness here together with development. Both are important. Wild places provide a soul-reviving interest. Just knowing that wild places exist is important for people. There is also comfort to be found in buildings. Yet, I know buildings and wilderness often can't be combined without developments eliminating the wilds.

Both Hunter and Seth were asleep before the setting sun infused red tints into a bluish haze, coloring the forest with a purple hue. Night's shadows were faded by light from an ocher moon. At daybreak, Seth washed in a rivulet of water. It tumbled down the side of a rock face then flowed toward the river.

Seth prepared coffee. He also heated a can of beans and shared them with Hunter. Both travelers were eager to continue the journey. Hunter checked the trail first followed by Seth who traveled slowly although steadily. The route, winding across a verdant land, was marked in time by camping places that eventually brought the travelers back to the truck.

Upon seeing the familiar outline of his truck appear amid foliage and tree trunks, Sethrum's thoughts returned to all the things he had to do. He suddenly felt a sense of urgency regarding a need to carry out his plans as soon as possible. Without delay, he returned Hog Hunter to Sihoki who started him on his last races. Having looked after the dog, Seth rented the same room at the Blue Heron Motel.

Sethrum sat on the chair located on his balcony. He sipped draft beer while watching a timeless pattern of waves crashing along the beach's sand and rushing back to the sea. I seem to have started a fishing trip I can't stop, he told himself. However, I must get back to work up north or the resort will hire someone else to look after the place.

After the splashing surge of each wave upon the sand, sandpipers scurried to look for food in the water rushing back to the Gulf. Farther out from shore, backs of dolphins broke gracefully through the water's surface. Pelicans glided endlessly overhead as if all they could think about was fish and no amount of effort was too much to pick up even a small, glass minnow. Sethrum watched the intermingling of these ageless patterns. He noticed that the heron was standing on the same chimney. Resembling a streamlined gargoyle coming to life, the heron stretched out its broad wings and flew to the beach in front of the balcony. Seth threw out pieces of fillets. The heron and egret ate the food while a cloud of gulls screamed and gathered overhead. Seth had to go into his room and get more food for the gulls.

The setting sun painted the horizon with golden hues. These tints gradually turned pink before deepening to scarlet then crimson. Having turned crimson itself, the sun descended through a purple haze to finally vanish leaving behind a remnant wisp of red light.

Next morning, the waiting heron and egret received more pieces of fillet. Afterward, Sethrum went to the beach and waded in the water bordering the shore. This area, including a sand bar, teemed with life. The usual shells were abundant along with a drifting cloud of stingrays. A school of glass minnows divided to let Sethrum pass through. Farther out, sleek shapes of Spanish mackerel moved through green depths while seeking minnows. All creatures—even fish—seemed to be looking for fish, said Sethrum to himself.

Sethrum returned to his room to assemble his fishing equipment. Upon

Pelican Moon

returning to the beach, he used his net to catch scaled sardines to use for bait. He baited his line and in a short time caught a ladyfish. He put this slender fish on his shark line. He completed these preparations and was left with his preferred task of watching both his fishing pole and the greenish-blue water of the Gulf. Out in deeper water, jacks thrashed at the surface while chasing sardines. Nothing hit Seth's line.

Each day, Seth did some fishing while he waited and watched the sky. Eventually, clouds brought steady rain on a day when Hog Hunter would be racing.

Rain splashed against the truck and its windshield during Sethrum's trip to the dog track. He parked his truck and the rain seemed to increase in intensity as he ran to the entrance of the building. He purchased a program along with some beer before going to his usual chair.

Wind driven rain pounded the track. This weather looks great, thought Seth while he checked his program. Sihoki says dogs running next to the inside rail have an advantage on a wet track. Hog Hunter has heart. He could even be the fastest on a wet track.

According to the program, Hunter was in the third race. Dogs numbered one and two, running next to the rail, were listed as being fast although two was better than one. Hunter was number eight and not a favorite.

Seth decided to place one trifecta bet. He listed Hunter to come in first. Dog, number two, was listed to come in second while listing dog, number one, to be third. Will's money would be used to get two additional tickets for will and Sihoki. All three tickets would have the same numbers, eight, two and then one.

I always like to aim high even though I might fail, Seth told himself on the way to the betting area. He purchased the three, trifecta tickets, followed by more beer, before returning to his chair.

During the first two races, the rain and wind threw off the results. Very little happened as indicated by the program. Losers were numerous. Because of the odds, high payments went to those who did win.

Leadouts walked the dogs for the third race. Seth got so excited he ran to get another large cup of beer. When he returned, the dogs were in the starting gate.

Wind driven rain pelted the track. Strains of music wandered with the wind. Dogs barked sharply then there was an eerie silence broken only by the whirring of wind combined with a hissing sound of rain splashing against the building and track. A mechanical rabbit approached the starting gate.

When the rabbit passed the gate, the dogs rushed in pursuit, moving so swiftly their shapes blurred into one speeding form with numerous legs splashing forward.

At the clubhouse turn, the greyhounds bunched together more closely then two dogs tumbled to the right. They stayed in the race although were behind the others that had broken into two groups.

The first bunch appeared to have the numbers three, two, one and eight. They stayed together until a sprawling splash caused a dog to swerve out and fall behind the others. Three was leading, followed closely by two. One ran right behind eight although all four dogs stayed in a group.

Watching the splashing onrush, Seth was gripped by excitement as he saw three fall behind the others. Seth froze when Hunter moved ahead, crossing the finish line in front of two and one. The dogs behind Hunter were so closely bunched there would be a delayed, photo finish.

Seth remained in a spell of excitement. As long as the winning numbers did not appear, he had not lost; so he did not mind waiting. Even if I don't win, he told himself, the risk has been worth everything. I know I can't keep winning or coming this close. I've had good information about Hunter. Even such information might not lead to winnings. One way or another, I'll start losing.

The winning numbers, eight, two and one, flashed on the board. Excitement pulsed through Seth while he stared at the numbers. Such a thing can't happen, he said to himself. Yet it has happened. I'm not going to question good fortune when it comes. It doesn't come all the time, so I'm just going to savor this turn of events. I'll give Sihoki and Will their winnings. I must also get back to work. Maybe now I can buy the resort.

Sethrum drove to the motel. He enjoyed its ocean-centered rhythms. This place has an appeal that's irresistible, he observed. Each time I come here, I wonder why I've been away so long.

The heron added its stately silhouette to the chimney while occasionally gliding to the beach to get a meal. Seth returned to his routines of fishing and shelling. When he realized he couldn't delay any longer, he packed his equipment, threw pieces of fillets to the birds then reluctantly left the motel and drove to the swamp.

Sihoki, Will and Hog Hunter were all present when Seth arrived at their home beside the river. Sihoki and Will were shocked by their winnings. "Lightning does strike the same place twice sometimes," exclaimed Will, amazed at his share of the money. "But don't expect a third strike," he added.

Sihoki served biscuits and coffee while Will checked a kennel behind the house. He was followed back to the house by a gangly, black and tan pup. "I'd like you to meet Cougar," said Will to Seth. "Cougar is one of Hunter's pups. I don't know if you need a dog; but you've got one now. Let him get accustomed to you slowly. When he sits down beside you by his own choice, you will have made a loyal friend."

"That's more than I could expect," exclaimed Sethrum. "He's greatly appreciated." Running his hand along the side of the dog's head, Seth said, "He'll be well looked after."

"We know," said Sihoki. "You'll be well looked after too," she added with a sparkle in her eyes.

Cougar was accustomed to riding in a truck. He seemed to accept the situation when Seth drove away from the home beside the river. I know where I'm going so well now I don't need maps, thought Seth. But the route I think I will take does not seem to be the same one that Sihoki sees ahead of me. Maybe there's nothing in what she says. However, I wish I wasn't so certain she knows exactly what she's doing regarding the spiritual journey she says I'm now starting.

SEVEN

<u>FOXWOOD</u>

During the drive north, Cougar sat on the front, passenger seat. They crossed the Canadian border and continued northward until most cities had been left behind, replaced by wilderness.

While he drove the truck, Sethrum turned his previously vague plans into definite forms. I've been an handy man at the Foxwood Resort which was once owned by a member of my family, Sethrum said to himself. With my dog track winnings, I can now buy this resort. In the south, I've seen development work side by side with wilderness. I'll see if I can implement this idea at the resort. I will probably run into the usual opposition. Some people will say I can develop anything I want but not in their wilderness. I'll need partners, probably including Katherine and Phil Dobbs. They will want to have something to do anyway after I buy the resort from them. Upstream, on the eastern side of our Fox River, I would like to start a condominium complex. I could also turn the resort itself into condominiums. I will call my project the Fox Condominium Company. I could offer luxurious accommodation and wilderness in one package. I've seen this idea work. I'll put it into operation at the Fox River. Maybe the time is right to bring development to the Fox River. That's my plan anyway.

Shadows of evening were lengthening and robins were singing when Seth's truck turned onto the driveway leading to the Foxwood Resort. He drove passed the Dobbs' house and office, proceeded down an hill then went north along a lane way behind cabins bordering the Fox

River. The truck stopped beside the last cabin. Seth opened the back door of his home. Cougar eagerly entered the building. Seth used a switch next to the door to turn on a light hanging from the ceiling. "Well Cougar, we're home," said Seth to the dog. "My equipment is all here; so I guess I haven't been fired during my absence."

The cabin was compact. A basic kitchen was located in the northeast corner. Along the remainder of the north wall, there were chairs located beneath a window. Other windows were on each side of a front door facing west toward the river. Next to the south wall, an Hudson Bay blanket covered a cot. A bathroom was located in the southeast corner. In the center of the main room, there was a wood stove. Piled next to it, was a good supply of firewood along with kindling.

Sethrum lit a fire in the stove. Next, he removed a bear rug from a trunk at the foot of the cot. He stretched out the rug on the floor beside this chest. Immediately recognizing his place in the cabin, Cougar came over and sat down on the black hide. To the dog, Seth said, "I bought this fur from bear hunters at Spirit Lake up the Fox River. I could've gone hunting to get my own rug; but I'm a fisherman, not an hunter. Before the fly season starts I'll take you by canoe to Spirit Lake."

When Cougar was asleep on his new bed, Seth put a pan of food next to him along with a bowl of water. Afterward, Seth rested on the cot. In a short time he too was asleep. He woke up in the gray light of dawn. A melodious chorus of robins' songs rang through the forest and filled the cabin. This harmony was broken briefly by raucous calls of grackles protecting their nest from marauding crows.

Seth started the day by opening a can of special, dog food for Cougar. Next, bacon and eggs were fried, followed by the preparation of coffee. A fire

Pelican Moon

pounding in the wood stove kept the cabin dry as well as warm. Outside, the day was gray and cold. New leaves forming on trees colored the forest with pastel shades of red, green and yellow. Robins continued to sing occasionally along with a thrasher.

After breakfast, Sethrum and Cougar left the cabin and started walking to the resort's office. Cougar immediately treed two of the owner's cats. Cougar looked pleased with himself when Seth said, "Good dog. Those cats are always out killing something."

The resort owners, Phil and Katherine Dobbs, invited Seth and Cougar into a spacious room that was well heated by a fire in a stone fireplace located in the southwest corner. Phil was a frail, mild-mannered man who had sad, brown eyes. His reddish moustache did not match his brown, thick, ill-fitting toupee. His wife, Katherine, represented more of the rooster in the family. Her eyes were dark and severe.

She kept her brown hair well combed and tied tightly at the back as if she liked to have everything about her and her life to be firmly in place. She carried herself erectly like a rooster trying to show off its dominance. "We wondered if you were coming back," she said accusingly to Seth after he sat down on a chair facing the fire. Phil served each person coffee while cougar stretched out on the floor beside Seth's chair.

"There's a lot o' work to do around here," added Phil, backing up his wife.

Phil and Katherine have done well with the business, thought Seth as he warmed his hands on the coffee cup. They do well because they move with the flow of events. They don't stand in the way of anything and they like any idea if it's profitable. I must appeal to their way of seeing things. "I brought back a new idea for you," said Seth after he had sipped the warming coffee. "My idea's profitable just like the business you have developed here. A long time ago, this area was completely a wilderness, visited by Algonkian and Huron hunters. The Mohawks extended a northern village to Spirit Lake. French fur traders traded with the Algonkians and Hurons while the Dutch, followed by the English, traded with the Mohawks and other nations of the League of Six Nations. These two trading and military alliances competed for this land. Loggers arrived later and put in the bush road that follows the old, Mohawk path up the eastern side of Fox River. One of my relatives started a trading post here. The hunt cabin was added later. Such beginnings developed into the resort we today call Foxwood. Your family bought this place. You have done well by changing with the times. I have kept up my family's interest by helping to look after the place."

When Seth stopped talking to drink the last of the coffee in his cup, Phil said, "Excuse me for a minute." He went to the kitchen, got the coffeepot and refilled the cups. He replaced the pot and returned to his chair.

"Thanks for the coffee," said Seth. "If you keep refilling my cup, I might never shut up."

"We're almost out o' coffee," replied Phil as a rare smile lit his face.

"When I was on my shark fishing holiday in the south," continued Seth, "I won money at the dog races. If we can come to an agreement, I would like to buy this place. You could continue to be managers. I will remain in the same cabin and be the handy man."

Phil looked at his wife to see if the idea was any good. Seth drank fresh coffee before continuing to say, "In the south, I saw the idea of wilderness and luxurious development working side by side. Just north o' here, at the old, hunt cabin site, we could build condominiums where people could come to enjoy the wilderness while, at the same time, live in luxury. If this plan

Pelican Moon

works, we could keep building and completely turn Foxwood into a condominium complex. We can take over the Fox River and Spirit Lake region. We will form the Fox Condominium Company. You must know other people who would become our partners to help finance this enterprise. While you are considering these ideas, I'm going to take Cougar on a canoe trip up the Fox River to Spirit Lake. I'm going to leave right away to avoid the black flies that will soon be with us."

Seth was relieved to stop talking. He had not said so much at one time for quite a while. Phil poured more coffee. His loosely fitting toupee gave him an insincere look. Katherine's tightly combed hair increased her stern appearance. Phil took the coffeepot back to the kitchen. When he returned, he added a piece of wood to the fire before he sat down. Flames crackled as they swarmed across the dry wood. A tendril of aromatic smoke curled into the room then vanished.

"We would sell this place to you if the price was right," stated Katherine, surprising her husband as well as Seth. "We've always had selling in mind. I'm also sure we would become partners with you in the new Condominium Company. We can get more partners. There's money to be made in development and condominiums are the way to go now. We might as well make the money as let someone else do it."

"When Seth is up the Fox River," offered Phil, "Katherine and I could get the paperwork and groundwork ready."

So that's the way things operate here, thought Seth. Katherine makes the decisions then Phil does much of the background work, putting the plans into action.

"It's time this place was developed anyway," stated Katherine caustically. "The bugs and trees have had their day."

"You have some things to get ready," said Seth before he stood up. Cougar got up, stretched led the way to the door.

"We'll be ready for business by the time you get back," said Katherine. After opening the door so Cougar could leave first, Seth stepped outside. Katherine walked to the open doorway and asked, "You aren't going to be away long, are you?"

"No," answered Seth. "We'll see you soon."

"We'll be ready," said Katherine before she closed the door. Seth followed Cougar and they quickly returned to the cabin.

While packing for a canoe trip up the Fox River, Seth stopped to look at the surrounding forest. Sometimes, he cautioned himself, I'm not completely certain about my own plans. Katherine agreed with my idea so easily that I wonder if I'm on the right track. I have seldom agreed with her in the past.

Daniel Hance Page

I like the idea of buying Foxwood because my family started a trading post here then the business expanded to become the Foxwood Resort. The condominium scheme will be profitable. Katherine has a good nose for a profit. She can smell a bargain at twenty miles the way a bear can smell a fish. Katherine and Phil know when to turn in order to keep in the trend of business. Maybe an idea that works in one place won't work in another. Some people will say development is all right but not in their wilderness—not in their neck o' the woods. There's much I don't know. That's what people keep telling me anyway. I should have talked more with Sihoki. People like her are not taken seriously enough. I also know I should start the river trip before black flies make traveling more difficult. Everyone has favorite localities. My favorite places are Spirit Lake and the Fox River.

EIGHT

THE RIVER

Sethrum Moon pushed his canoe onto the Fox River. He held the canoe while Cougar jumped inside and sat in the bow. The dog was always very much aware of surrounding scents, sounds and sights. He watched ripples left by a splashing fish. Expanding ripples covered the place where a snapping turtle's head had slipped beneath the surface.

From resting places on an half submerged log next to shore, two mud turtles watched the man step into the stern of the canoe. A cardinal's song rang through the forest as the paddle dipped into the cold, tea-colored water. The craft surged forward beside the east bank. A vulture watched from a stand of ash trees. Other vultures circled silently overhead. Farther upstream, sea gulls called. A pair of mergansers moved away from the path of the canoe as it rounded a bend and proceeded passed an occupied beaver lodge.

Cougar watched a fish swirling the water's surface in front of the old, hunt camp. This is where my project will start, thought Seth upon seeing a weathered building located a short distance from the water. I'll build condominiums here before expanding to replace Foxwood. People can come here to experience the wilderness while enjoying luxurious accommodation.

Rhythmically, the paddle dipped into dark water, pushing the craft farther upstream between banks stirring with new life that comes with springtime. The forest's floor was mottled by yellowish-green stands of stately, fiddlehead ferns along with yellow patches of swamp marigolds and dogtooth violets in addition to white and purple trilliums. New leaves on trees supplied a background blend of pastel colors, particularly yellow, green and red.

At the first rapids, large spawning suckers thrashed around rocks protruding from tumbling water. Tired fish rested in shallow pools. Vultures ripped meat from dead fish along the rocky banks. Screaming gulls circled above the area. The birds and fish were pushed into further action by the intrusion of the man and dog.

After jumping from the canoe, Cougar rushed through shallow water and entered a pool rippled by backs of resting fish. The water erupted as frenzied suckers tried to escape from the attacking dog. Cougar clamped his jaws on a struggling fish, carried it out of the water then returned for another. The first fish to be removed had on its back marks from a bear's teeth.

Sethrum carried his canoe and packs around the rapids. Cougar reluctantly stopped fishing and took his place in the bow. Seth sat in the stern and was pleased to start paddling again, pushing the craft steadily upstream into an unusually flat, swampy area. The banks were low and topped by gnarled willows. One aged willow had fallen across the river, forcing Seth to make another portage.

Beyond the log portage, he followed the river between verdant, fern-covered banks that often contained smooth rocks and were crested by lofty, white pines with branches etched against an azure sky. Rocks increased along the banks until rock walls pushed the river into a long, cascading rapids.

For the third time, Sethrum had to carry his canoe. Beyond the rapids, the channel opened to the normal width of the river. He returned to get his packs and had to wait while Cougar chased more suckers. When Cougar attacked, the fish thrashed in a frenzied rush to escape from a shallow pool.

Pelican Moon

In the normal width of river above the channel, Seth enjoyed the routine of paddling. With each stroke of the paddle, he steered the craft and pushed it forward without having to think much about each required maneuver. He reached a short section of rapids and had to portage again. Afterward, there was easy paddling over a long expanse of unobstructed water.

The sky was receiving yellow colors from the setting sun when the canoe came to an area where the green-tinged stream flowed down a natural stairway of wide, smooth rocks. Shafts of sunlight dropping through openings in a canopy of branches added gold wedges to green hues in the water as it moved over smooth rocks. At the bottom of each ledge, water splashed into white crests before swirling onward to the next drop. Beside this emerald waterway, Seth first carried his canoe then the packs while Cougar looked for fish.

Above the rapids, on the eastern side of the river, there was a rocky hill. Seth pulled his canoe onto smooth rocks on the bank and found this elevated area to be a natural camping site he had not paid much attention to during previous trips. Near the rock summit, other travelers had used stones to construct an horseshoe-shaped fireplace topped by a grill. Each time I revisit a river, reflected Seth, there are new things to discover. Even the remembered places change with different water levels or alterations in beaver dams. Each journey, even over old territory, is a new experience.

Seth made camp while a golden sunset faded, bringing deepening hues of evening around a brightening fire. A tent was positioned back from the fire. A tarpaulin extended from the tent to the fire's edge. A propane lantern provided a steady source of light to the site. The still evening rang with the calls of spring peepers. Above the fire, steaks were roasted for Seth and Cougar. Afterward, coffee was perked and Seth sipped it slowly while he rested and enjoyed the accomplishment of having made a comfortable camp in rugged surroundings.

The high, rock camp provided a view of the stairway falls downstream along with a swath of calm water upstream. Ferns carpeted humus next to camp. Firelight danced across bald rocks before dropping to the river. Occasionally a fish's back or tail rippled the water's calm surface. An heron stalked a reedy section along the far bank. In the distance, a wolf howled.

Seth watched an orange moon. It first flashed fire-like light through foliage then seemed to disentangle itself from trees before rising above the forest. The orange color slowly drained away leaving a silver orb in a starlit sky. Moonlight shone upon the river turning it into a swath of light slashed through the forest. A fish jumped in silver spray. Ripples from the fish's leap lingered until they were cut by the bows of two canoes.

A warning growl came from Cougar. He walked to the water's edge and barked while four people pulled two canoes up onto the bank beside Seth's craft. The strangers, in single file, started climbing the hill.

"What do you want?" demanded Seth. His voice rang loudly through the moonlit night. He did not like being outnumbered, at night, in the wilderness. He had an uneasy feeling and uncased his rifle.

"This is our campsite," stated a woman's voice. It came from the largest of the four people. She had advanced well ahead of the others.

"It's occupied," stated Seth.

"We're just visiting then," answered the woman.

"Okay," said Seth. "Do you always visit people at night in the woods?"

"No," she replied. "This is the first time anyone else has ever been here." Firelight outlined the features of a strong, robust woman with shortly cropped brown hair and black, lively eyes. She seemed to be the leader of the group.

The second person to step into light from the camp, was a slim woman with long, dark hair and brown eyes. She seemed willing to let the other woman do the talking. Two men lurked in the background. One man was of average, although slightly overweight, stature. He had short, dark hair, wore glasses and appeared to be an easy-going type. The other man was small and wiry. He had medium length, blond hair and a darker, longish moustache beneath a jutting as well as pointed nose. He looked like he might be a lecturer or a speaker of some kind. This man's gaze darted quickly from one part of the camp to another and did not notice the rifle that had been slipped inside the tent's doorway.

"We won't be any bother," said the large woman. "We'll just rest here for a while, if you don't mind, then we'll keep traveling. We've camped here often."

"The place was clean when I got here," said Seth.

"And it still is clean," said the same woman. "That's good to see."

"Do you have two cups?" asked Seth while he removed two cups from his pack.

"Yeah, we do," she answered while opening a pack she had been carrying.

"I carry two extras," said Seth as he prepared four cups of coffee with side jars of creamer and sugar. Having refilled the pot with water and ground coffee, he replaced this blackened pot on the grill to perk then all the people sat down around the fire.

"Who are you?" the large woman asked directly.

"Seth Moon," he answered. "Who are you?"

Pointing to the woman next to her, the talkative woman said, "Taisse Cantry." Indicating the overweight man, she said, "Paul Kimbal." Pointing to the other man, she said, "Over there, we have Redge Sims. I'm Sal Perkins. We're members of the Wild Society. We're coming back from checking two hunt camps at Spirit Lake. The spring bear hunt is on now. We're against hunting of any kind. But at least the hunters at the west camp keep the place clean and are careful about what they're doing. They don't just shoot up the place, leaving wounded animals behind along with lots o' garbage. At the eastern end o' the lake, there's an entirely different situation. Bear hunters left that camp just recently. We went in and cleaned up the mess, bringing out five bags o' garbage. At this early part of the season guns can't be used for bear hunting. Hunting has to be done with a bow and arrow; so there's an increased chance of animals getting away wounded."

While listening to Sal, Sethrum thought about the rifles he had seen on top of equipment in the canoes. Each visitor had a knife in a sheath attached to a belt. Paul and Redge seemed to be quiet people, content to let Sal do most of the talking. I think the women are the leaders of this group, Sethrum told himself. The slim woman has black hair and light brown eyes. She doesn't try to adorn her natural beauty.

"We had so much work to do to clean up that eastern camp we were late leaving. We can get back quickly from here. Even at night we know the way. There's so much moonlight tonight we can see where we are going even along the rapids."

"What else does the Wild Society do?" asked Seth.

"We try to preserve the wilderness," answered Sal. "We want remaining wilderness areas to be protected."

"People have to be able to see the forest," said Seth.

"Yes, they do," agreed Sal. "They just don't have to wreck it. We are using this river now; but we're not destroying it."

"We can have development without wrecking wild places," countered Seth.

"Yes," she said, "that's possible in some ways in some places. However, certain regions should never be touched. This Fox River area is one place that must stay as it is."

"Are you always so definite?" asked Seth.

"You only get wilderness once," added Taisse.

"Studies have shown," said Redge, "that more money can be made from a preserved wilderness than from an area that is allowed to be destructively logged or otherwise ruined. Careful logging doesn't wreck a forest. Clear cutting removes the wilderness. There is nothing left except ruined land or maybe a tree farm. In a tree farm, all trees are planted at the same time. As a result, the trees grow at the same height and block out sunlight from all things below the top canopy. Beneath the top foliage, there is a type of dead forest."

"You can have wilderness and development together," countered Seth. He was starting to feel uneasy about what seemed to be an approaching confrontation.

"Yes, you can have wilderness and development together," replied Sal. "That's not going to happen here, however. Some wilderness areas have to be preserved as they are. If the trend doesn't stop somewhere, wilderness people will run out of places to go. This happens to be our place. I get interested in issues when they become personal. People can have development but not in my wilderness. We're not moving. Other people can leave."

"I'm working on a plan to build luxury accommodations at Foxwood to open up this area so people can make use of it," said Seth, feeling increasingly tense.

"It's being used now at its very best," stated Taisse pleasantly yet definitely. "If you spoil this place, it will never be useful at its best again."

"Your plan is workable but not here," said Redge Sims.

"We don't want to lose timeless beauty and interest," said Taisse. "I like to be able to walk where previous people have walked. I want to have a chance to see the land as they saw it. With too many changes, we lose what the land was and is. In the real world, the spiritual world, all things are connected and we don't want our forest ruined. Some places can be developed. Other regions are best just as they are.

We don't want the Fox River area changed. Development and wilderness can be good but not everywhere. We have to keep some places just as they are and this river is one of those areas."

Seth served more coffee; yet there was a tense feeling in the camp. Each person was accustomed to talk around a campfire being jovial. However, this night's conversation had hit an impasse. "We aren't opposing all development," said Paul Kimbal in an effort to be pleasant. "A mix of city and wilderness can be good. On the other hand, there are places where development must not intrude. Some areas must remain as they have always been. We have marked the Fox River as a wilderness area. Indian nations have lived here. There was a Mohawk village at the eastern side of Spirit Lake in about 1720. Since that time, fur traders, trappers, hunters and some loggers have been here. None of these people really altered the place.

Construction on a large scale would bring much more loss than gain."

"This place is wild and nothing's going to change," stated Redge, turning the tension up another notch.

"I guess that's what we're all trying to say," added Sal.

"What work do you do?" Taisse asked Seth.

"I work at Foxwood," he answered. "I think I just bought the place."

"We launch our canoes just north of there," said Redge.

"North of the resort, at the old, cabin site, we are going to start building a condominium complex," replied Seth, knowing that trouble was coming so he might as well face it.

His statement was met by silence around the campfire. Spring peepers called from the river. A wolf howled in the distance. The fire snapped as the flames danced light across serious faces. Seth watched Taisse in the shadows. She's intriguingly beautiful, he said to himself. *Yet she looks like a mystery that will move farther away each time I try to understand her.*

"You're kidding," snapped Sal.

Feeling increasingly uneasy, Seth said directly, "People can enjoy easy living at our center which will also put them in the wilderness. Our company will use this river for regular trips. This development is coming. Get used to it."

Seth noticed the grimaces marking the faces of the people in the firelight before Sal said, "You've got a good idea. It just isn't a good idea for this wild place. Such things as you propose must be kept from here to preserve this river's original beauty."

"Some of our members aren't as reasonable as we are," added Redge.

"My plan will work," replied Seth, noting Redge's warning. "I've seen it work."

"The wilderness already works," stated Redge. "It works best just the way it is without your meddling. I like this area just the way it is. Every year there are fewer of these areas. Less and less people have an opportunity to see such a sight. Your plan would ruin the view so the real beauty would be gone by the time your visitors got here."

"I've seen the plan work in other places," countered Seth, knowing that both sides had stopped listening to each other.

"Yes, but not here," stated Redge.

"Maybe we should be going," said Paul.

"Maybe we should," said Taisse. She stood up, put her coffee cup on a rock near the fire and started walking down the hill toward the canoes. Sal was the next to leave the camp, followed by Redge and Paul.

The four people were soon paddling their two canoes downstream. They moved out of view at the approach to the stairway falls.

"I guess I said all the wrong things," Seth said to Cougar. "Sometimes I think I understand the wilderness more than people. But someone like Taisse can cause a fellow a lot of discontentment, even with the wilderness. I think this affect has already started."

Seth went into his tent and welcomed the warmth as well as the comfort of the sleeping bag on its springy mattress of boughs. Cougar stretched out on a sheepskin vest. Moonlight dropped through a screened window. Looking at the tent's compact interior, Seth thought, Algonkians and Hurons hunted here. Mohawks had a northern village at the eastern end of Spirit Lake in 1720. French voyageurs came here to trade with Algonkians and Hurons. English traders and missionaries visited the Mohawks. The French, Algonkians and Hurons were periodically at war with the English and Six Nations including the Mohawks. Loggers came to this area. Because they used horses to move logs, the forest was not ruined. Hunters visited and are still here. Previous visitors have not basically altered the region. The Wild Society wants to preserve this area as it is now and has been. I have the plan of building a condominium complex to bring people here to enjoy the wilderness. There's opposition; yet there are always obstacles. The bigger the plan, the greater are the difficulties. The Wild Society members have their opinions. I'll stick to mine.

NINE

SPIRIT LAKE

Sethrum Moon was awakened at dawn by robins' songs. While this ringing melody brought the forest to life, shafts of sunlight illuminated spring foliage on trees before reaching carpets of ferns and patches of trilliums in addition to dogtooth violets. Water flowing over smooth rocks carried tints of green and yellow that became added to spray at the base of ledges. Paths of sunlight shooting through foliage connected the colors of sky, land and water.

There is so much beauty here, noted Sethrum as he emerged from his tent. I've always felt at home with the rocks, trees and river. I enjoyed being alone here until I met Taisse. After seeing her beauty, I could become discontented with the wilderness. The Wild Society wants to leave the wilderness in its natural state. I plan to use the wild and put it to work. The Society seems to think my way of using the forest would take away its wildness.

After adding water to a pancake batter, Seth poured this batter into an hot, oiled frying pan. The mixture cooked quickly and was flipped over to the other side. It soon turned to the same golden color. This thick pancake was cut in half so both Seth and Cougar could enjoy a good breakfast. Coffee was also perked.

Following breakfast, the camp equipment was packed and placed in the canoe. With Cougar in the bow, Sethrum pushed the craft out from shore then he stepped inside and took his comfortable, familiar place at the stern. Slipping into dark, golden water, the paddle pushed the craft forward. A few spring peepers called. A vulture watched from a dead tree. Mergansers took to flight. With a whir of wings, the birds moved steadily across the sky.

The canoe pushed forward. Each thrust of the paddle brought Seth into a new angle to a swath of river bordered by verdant banks. Lofty, white pines were silhouetted against a light, blue sky. Closely interlaced hemlock branches reached down to the water. Birches added pale, vertical slashes to the forest's predominantly green colors. Tall ferns topped the banks.

The water trail flowed between sandbanks then more rocky sections before coming to a low region. The river gradually widened until its eastern bank swept away to become the eastern shoreline of Spirit Lake. The western bank turned sharply west to form a long, narrow lake.

The eastern shoreline was a flat area of rustling grasses. Seth paddled to

Pelican Moon

the north point where the Fox River entered the lake. He proceeded up this entering stream and came to a bog. It was the source of the river. Water bubbled out from under grassy banks. Looking over the grass-covered land at the lake's eastern end, Seth said to himself, the Mohawk village was here in 1720. This place is as beautiful now as it was then.

Sethrum paddled to smooth rocks at the north shore of the lake. Eastward, there was the river's inlet on the flat land. This area would have been used by the old village to grow corn, beans, squash and tobacco, observed Seth. Looking south, he could see the wide path of the river's outlet. Westward was the long, narrow lake. It was just an extreme widening of the river.

Detecting the presence of a path leading away from the water at the eastern shoreline, Seth paddled back to this shore. He hauled his canoe onto a level area where the grass had been trampled and other canoes had been placed recently.

Cougar charged ahead along the path and Seth followed as closely as possible. While almost running to try to keep Cougar in sight, Seth thought, this trail must lead to the camp of the destructive hunters that the Wild Society people were complaining about.

A gray silhouette of a cabin came into view amid bushes. The structure was a square-shaped shack with sloppily built additions on the north and south ends. Boards covered the windows. East of the shack, sea gulls called. Broad winged vultures circled overhead. Seth and Cougar went to see what was attracting the birds and found a reeking pile of suckers guarded by a cloud of flies. Fish are used as bait to attract bears, noted Sethrum as he saw the tree platform where an hunter would wait. Mohawks settled here without taking away this area's beauty. Fur traders did not ruin the place. The wilderness continues after loggers have been here and hunters. None of these groups ended the chain of beauty. Although some of them were destructive, not one of them severed the link to the past. So far, no one has taken away the genuine wilderness from the next people to come here. When links to the past are not cut, we can go back more easily. Sihoki said that in the spirit world a person is able to see the past, present and future. I would like to know what she saw ahead for me.

Cougar's sharp barks brought Seth's attention back to the camp. The dog was barking at something near the canoe. If someone steals my canoe, I'll be stuck here for a long time, Seth warned himself before he started running along the path leading to the lake.

The barking became more intense as if Cougar was locked in a battle. When Seth reached the water, he saw a bear circling—usually agilely, although sometimes awkwardly—and trying to fend off Cougar's swift attacks. The bear appeared to be wounded because it kept stumbling. The creature was also angry. It roared each time a paw shot forward and missed the dog. To avoid the flailing paw, Cougar retreated like a gust of wind only to strike again from a different angle.

Detecting a new danger, the bear stood up on its hind legs and sniffed the air. Taking advantage of an unguarded moment, Cougar dove in and back again staying away from a black paw as it raked the air causing the bear to growl with pain. An arrow's broken shaft protruded from the animal's side. A second shaft was lodged in the shoulder, rendering that front leg useless.

Following another furious swipe at the maddening dog, the black giant charged Seth. The animal ran in a stumbling gait. When Cougar attacked from behind, the bear sat down, turned around and shot a clawed paw toward this thing that could not be hit.

Giving up on Cougar, the bear turned its rage against Seth, charging while growling deeply. Gripped by cold fear, Seth picked up a chunk of wood. Mustering all his strength to protect himself from this raging animal, Seth slammed the wood against the creature's nose, stunning the attacker. Seth stepped beside the bear's damaged leg while the other paw raked the air. Roaring with anger, the great head swung from side to side. Blood spurted from the torn nose. A mixture of blood and saliva dripped from the mouth. Warm breath stank of rotten fish.

Cougar attacked from the back. When the giant's head turned to confront this constant irritation, Seth sank his knife under the bear's injured leg. The animal lurched and swiped its good paw with such speed Seth was knocked backwards into a thicket of alders. Instantly the bear was at him with blood spraying from the knife wound. This attack was broken again by Cougar. After swinging an arcing paw at the dog, the giant pitched headfirst to the ground and remained there with blood flowing from the knife wound.

Wobbling slightly due to weariness, Cougar followed Seth as he stumbled into the lake. He crawled into the numbingly cold water and let it soothe bruises and scrapes while offering relief from a pulsing headache. Seth turned over onto his back and rested in the encompassing chill. He watched clouds drifting slowly across a pale, blue sky. Silhouetted against the moving sky, there was the whiskered head of Cougar. The dog watched and waited.

Although bruises were large and joined by pain, Seth was relieved to determine that no bones had been broken. A long, numbing soak continued until a chill replaced the pain. Shaking from the cold, he left the water, got into the canoe with Cougar then paddled

Pelican Moon

westward. The wilderness is rugged and beautiful, Seth told himself. Yet people can do a lot of harm to this land. The destructive bear hunters didn't leave the wilderness as they found it.

Midway along the lake, Sethrum turned to the north shore where he hauled his canoe onto a flat rock. Behind this flat area, the rock reached upward to become topped by white pines. On this summit, there was a natural camping place. Seth camped here and welcomed a chance to rest and sleep.

Next morning, a calm lake reflected its surrounding shoreline as well as a mackerel sky. Sea gulls, wheeling overhead, started issuing a clamor of calls. Cougar watched a large, water snake slither down to the water and cut across its mirrored surface.

Sethrum's aches seemed to have fused together into an overall feeling of soreness accompanied by a slight dizziness. Another soaking in the frigid water soothed the pain in addition to awakening his mind and senses. After leaving the water, he built a tall fire. Its warmth removed a lingering chill that had settled into the core of his body. Cougar watched fish as they occasionally splashed on the lake's calm surface. From each disturbance, ripples expanded until they mixed with others to temporarily obliterate a reflected image of shoreline and sky. An heron flew above the lake, heading for a marshy area to the west. Resonant squawking calls echoed across the water.

Seth fried pancakes for himself and Cougar. Coffee was perked. Holding a cup of coffee, Seth sat down next to the fire and watched the lake. This is a mysterious place, he said to himself. People haven't changed it. I can sit here and be back in the times of the Algonkian hunters, Huron hunters, Mohawk villagers, fur traders, trappers, loggers and more recent hunters.

Sethrum pushed his canoe into the water and placed his equipment in the craft. Cougar took his usual place at the bow. Seth stepped inside and sat in the stern. Soreness worked its way out of his arms and back while he paddled. Extending westward, along the north shore, there were high rocks crested by white pines. The south shore was flat and swampy.

Upon reaching the western end of the lake, Seth saw a well used path leading down to the water. He paddled toward this path, bringing his canoe to shallow water next to the shore. Cougar jumped out of the bow before Seth stepped out of the craft. He pulled it onto a mossy section of the shore then proceeded to follow the path. Cougar led the way. Seth carried his rifle.

The melodious call of an ovenbird rang through a forest colored by green, yellow and red hues of new leaves. Trunks of birches added pale, vertical slashes to the greenery of pines, spruces and hemlocks. A ruffed grouse walked noisily on dry leaves. The well-camouflaged bird hid among ferns as Seth passed on the trail.

The hunt cabin fit neatly into the forest. Since the door was open, Cougar walked inside followed by Seth. The interior was clean. Shelves were stocked with cans of food. The wood stove was warm, containing glowing embers.

"Someone is around here," said Seth to Cougar. "There's no boat or canoe on the shore. If the people who lit this stove left by boat, we would've seen them. Someone has been left behind and is likely hunting."

Cougar had so many scents to check he had not selected one from the others. Slipping a rope leash around the dog's neck, Seth explained, "I don't want you chasing any more bears."

By keeping the leash loose, Seth allowed Cougar to detect the freshest scent to follow. It led to a rough trail which wound northwest into an high, rocky area topped by pines. "They're probably baiting bears back here," said Seth Softly to Cougar. The path became steep before reaching a level, rocky terrain with scrub brush.

Upon seeing the bear feeding at a pile of fish located on a flat rock, Seth tied Cougar's rope to a gnarled, jack pine. The bear was busy feeding and had not yet noticed a man approaching and carrying a short spear. Why would anyone look for trouble like that? Seth asked himself as he aimed his rifle at the bear. A scent or sound alerted the large, black form tearing at fish. The bear stood up and turned around just before the man lunged forward and drove his spear into the wide chest. Roaring with fury, the animal slapped at the shaft, splintering it. Almost as part of the same motion, the large bear sprang at the man and bounded after him.

Seth's first shot knocked the animal over into a leg-kicking tumble. Coming up again quickly, the dark form renewed its charge until a second shot dropped the creature headfirst onto rocks.

The bear did not move. Meanwhile, the man had started walking toward the source of the shots. Cougar pulled his head through the collar on the leash and bounded forward. He barked briefly at the approaching stranger before rushing onward to investigate the fallen bear.

The man circled back to retrieve a floppy hat containing an eagle feather. Starting to walk toward Seth again, this person wore the hat. It seemed to match the rest of his shaggy appearance. His hair was white and long like his beard. Pale blue eyes stared from under thick brows. Revealing crooked, stained teeth, he said, "Thanks for savin' my hide. I must admit I've never been so scared in all my life. That bear was so close I was expectin' his teeth to tear into my back. Those shots are the sweetest things I've ever heard. That spear trick was used in the old, loggin' camps. If you get a short spear into a bear's chest, the animal will strike at the pain and drive the shaft in farther. I've seen this thing done. The bear is killed quickly. I wasn't so lucky. You saved my life. I always thought I should try usin' the spear so I tried. I'll never do that again."

"I won't be tryin' that either," replied Seth. "I prefer to leave critters alone."

"You're right," he said good-naturedly. "That's where they should be left. We're huntin' bear. My grandsons took the boat back for fresh supplies. I get tired o' new things. I thought I'd try one of the old ways. Some of the old ways are foolish too. Who are you anyway?"

"Seth Moon," answered Seth. Pointing to the dog coming back after checking the bear, he said, "That's my dog, Cougar."

"I've never been so pleased to meet anyone," exclaimed the man who still could not believe his good luck. "I'm Sam Calley. Come on over to my cabin. I can get you some bear meat an' coffee."

"Thanks," said Seth as he turned to start following the man back to his cabin. Cougar walked ahead of Seth and behind Sam.

Inside the practical, yet comfortable, cabin, Cougar stretched out on the floor near the door. Seth sat on a homemade chair. Sam cooked while he talked. "Lot o' people are spooked by bears," he said. "Once you get the hide off a bear, it looks too much like an human. A bear walkin' in the woods sounds much like a person. Bears have a good sense o' smell although not such sharp eyesight or hearin'. A bear is as unpredictable as a bull-moose in the fall, rutting season."

Seth found the bear meat to be tender and tasty although a little bland.

Cougar liked the chunks he was given. The dog also received a pan of water before the men got coffee. "My dad told me to always look after your animals first," explained Sam. "Of course, he was talkin' about horses; but all animals should be cared for the same way. You can't mistreat animals or people. Although I do a little huntin', I consider that to be food gatherin'. Shooting for food is much different than unnecessarily hurting or wasting life. The most dangerous animal in the woods is a person. We hear about damage done by animals. However, there's nothin' like the harm done by people. The bush can take care o' itself without meddling from people. People never did know how to manage a forest."

After Seth and Sam moved away from the table and sipped coffee while sitting on chairs beside the wood stove, Sam said, "My grandsons have gone back for supplies, like beer."

"How do they get back?" asked Seth.

"They take my boat to the eastern end o' this lake. After hiding the boat in brush, they drive their all terrain vehicle along the old, Indian trail. It runs from the north to the south, same as the river. A car, or even a truck, can't use that lane. It takes an all terrain vehicle. The Indian trail connected with a Mohawk village that used to be at the eastern end o' this lake. A force of French and Algonkians attacked this village. The village moved south after a few years. Villages moved every ten to twenty years."

Sam refilled the cups then continued to say, "Your name is Seth Moon. When the Mohawk village was here, during the days o' the fur trade, the English traded with the Mohawks. An English trader had a cabin at Sky Mountain, north o' here. He traded with the Mohawk village. Maybe you're related to him because his name was Ridgeworth Moon."

"I'm related to Rid Moon," replied Seth. "He moved south and started a trading post that became Foxwood. An hunt camp was added later. My relatives ran both places and later sold the business to the Dobbs family. I just bought the place."

Seth sipped some strong coffee before asking, "Have you always lived around here?"

"Yeah," answered the man who was as roughly hewn as his cabin. "I've been a trapper, logger, fisherman, prospector and carpenter. Now I don't do much other than a little carpentry. I like this area and come here each year. I brought my grandsons with me this spring to hunt bear."

"Each person who comes here brings a story or finds one," observed Seth.

"No one has ruined the place yet," continued Sam who obviously could live alone yet he enjoyed company. "Everything is much the same as in 1720 when the Mohawk village was on the east shore. Those people had legends and visions. The year 1720 is remembered because at that time an army of Algonkians and French came up from the south along what we call today the Indian trail. This army camped beside the trail near a large beaver pond. An English trader warned the village about the attack. Some stories say he was Ridgeworth Moon or a trader working with Ridgeworth. Men from the village ambushed the army then pretended to retreat. The army advanced into a trap and got attacked from all sides. The enemy suffered a great defeat. The village was saved and prospered."

"A lot has happened at this lake," noted Seth.

"They say it's not just a lake and the river is not just a river," replied Sam. "Indian people have always come here for visions."

Seth was reminded of Sihoki and the coincidence of hearing this man talk about visions. "Are you bothered much by the Wild Society?" he asked.

"I actually get along quite well with them," replied Sam. "I might even be interested in joining them; but they can carry things too far. Taisse Cantry does the organizing while Sal Perkins does much of the talking. They cleaned up the hunt camp at the eastern end of this lake. They came here too for a visit. I served my standard meal o' bear meat and coffee. They're against hunting, although some of them are almost reasonable. They can cause a lot o' trouble too. They shot at hunters at the eastern camp. Loggers started working much farther east and were going to clear-cut in this direction until snipers shot at logging trucks and blew up their headquarters along with a bridge. That company went out o' business. The eastern hunters might not be back. The Wild Society often lives up to its name."

"They didn't like my idea of developing Foxwood, the hunt camp next to it and the Fox River, said Seth. "I would like to combine development with wilderness."

"No, I suppose the Society wouldn't be too supportive there," replied Sam as a wide smile revealed his uneven teeth. "I have seen development and wilderness together. A wild place can exist whether there's a road encircling the area or not. If you try to develop Fox River, you'll run up against some people like those in the Society. If a person wants to enjoy luxurious accommodation and wilderness also, such things can be found without difficulty. However, if a person prefers to enjoy a secluded, wild land in its original state, these regions are gettin' harder to find. This is the only secluded area I visit. There are other such places; but they're hard to find and becoming scarcer all the time. If someone built a road around this lake, I'd have to go and try to find another place like this is now. Since you saved me from the bear, I'll have to overlook your buildings. Watch out though for that Wild Society. My grandsons call them the Wild Bunch. They might talk politely at first. I warn you though that they're anything but polite once they take a dislike to someone."

Cougar got up and stretched. Seth said, "I appreciate your hospitality. However, I should be getting back to work. I have a Wild Society to stir up."

"Any time," answered Sam. "I enjoy company—unlike some of us that live alone in the woods. Thanks again for savin' my hide."

Seth stood up, saying, "I appreciated the meal." He and Sam followed Cougar and they all left the cabin. Upon reaching the lakeshore, Sam helped Seth slip the canoe into the water. Seth and Cougar took their usual positions. "Take care o' your hide," said Seth after he started to paddle. He moved the craft away from the shore and Sam said, "Watch the Wild Bunch."

Paddling steadily, Seth headed south then turned east. The shore was a mix of rock and lowland. Chokecherry trees were in blossom. Trilliums added purple and white colors to the forest's floor. Ravens called from a cloudy sky above the lake. Fragrances from blossoms scented the air in unseen streamers.

Sethrum paddled to the east shore where the old village had been located. Stopping beside flat rocks, he tried to visualize the place as it had been. This site is full of ghosts or just spirits maybe, he reflected. Sihoki said all spirits—and everything—are aspects of one spirit who is God.

Looking across the wide sweep of flat terrain, he said to himself, the river emerges from inside the boundary of the old village. Adjacent lands were fields for growing corn, beans and squash along with tobacco. The community was warned about an impending attack. Men went out, rushed along the trail and defeated the advancing army.

Occupied by thoughts of the past, Seth traveled down the Fox River. He paddled to a sandy section of the bank in front of the old, hunt cabin where his new complex would be started. Considering the possibility that he might have to leave in an hurry, he left his canoe at the water's edge. He removed the rifle from its case. I'm not quite as outnumbered when I'm carrying my rifle, he told himself. Under a mackerel sky, painted with reds and pinks by the setting sun, he accompanied Cougar to the cabin. The structure had been built with logs. Brush near the building partly concealed the Wild Society's canoes. Light illuminated a window on each side of the door facing the river.

The Wild Bunch has been using my cabin, said Seth to himself before he opened the door. He entered a large room where a fire blazed in a stone fireplace occupying much of the east wall. Couches were located along the south and west walls.

Leaving the front room, Seth and Cougar walked through an open doorway located on the south side of the fireplace. A short hallway led to a room containing bunk beds on the south side and a kitchen to the north. In the kitchen, a large man had just removed a bottle of beer from a refrigerator. He was turning around while unscrewing a cap from the bottle when his eyes focused on the advancing form of Cougar. Issuing an high pitched scream, the man kicked at the dog. Although Cougar sprang to one side, he yelped shrilly as the boot grazed the side of his head. He flashed back with disarming speed, sinking teeth through jeans above the boot. Growling deeply, Cougar swung his head from side to side and started tearing away a long chunk of material. The man lost his balance and fell backwards, yelling, "Help me! A dog's got me!"

The man's free leg shot out a sharp kick, causing Cougar to lose his grip. Seth leveled a rifle at the man while Cougar started tearing off a section from the fellow's jacket. He screamed again for help.

Two men scrambled in through a back doorway. Seth fired a shot over their heads. The blast exploded through the inside of the building, shocking the men but they kept moving forward. Seth swung his rifle, scraping its barrel across the closest man's jaw. The second man rocked Seth with a solid punch above his eye. Seth was dazed. As his sight was clearing, he saw Taisse Cantry's boot shoot up toward his crotch before pain flashed through him. The pain burned into anger. He swung the gun in a circling motion, driving the people backwards. He blasted a shot above the doorframe. The shot was deafening in the enclosed space. "It's time for you to leave," Seth told the people crowding the doorway. "I'm going to fill this area with new buildings."

A large man came from outside and pushed his way passed the others. He had an hulking, muscular form that moved confidently as if he was accustomed to not being stopped.

Cougar's hair stood up on his neck. A vicious snarl tore from his throat. He saw the kick and grabbed the boot with teeth that cut into leather. When Seth's gun butte hit the man's jaw, he toppled over backwards. With Cougar continuing to fight the boot, the man pulled himself to the doorway where he was replaced by two of his friends. They had just entered the building and attacked immediately. Seth connected a punch to one man's face, knocking him over onto his back. The second man doubled Seth over with a blow to the stomach. Gasping for air, he swung his rifle at the next oncoming fist. This man screamed and used his good hand to hold his bleeding fist then shot an unexpected uppercut against Seth's jaw. Dazed again, Seth pulled back. Cougar moved swiftly to Seth's side. The dog's teeth continued to hold a long piece of leather. It swung like a dead snake from victorious jaws. Seth moved toward the hallway and Cougar remained at his side while growling menacing at the other sullen, approaching people. Stepping away more quickly, Seth, followed by Cougar, reached the front doorway and rushed outside. "We've had enough for now," said Seth to Cougar. The dog kept shaking a strip of boot.

Seth followed Cougar to the canoe and they both got inside quickly. After paddling to a grassy section of the bank, Seth stepped out of the canoe, tied it to an overhanging branch then lowered himself into the chilling water. When he was up to his neck in the numbing water, he rested and let the cold soothe his pains while he watched the river's calm surface. Mist stirred above the stream. A quacking call of a duck cut loudly through the night. Splashing sounds followed. A muskrat swam on the surface before diving to murky depths. After a last flip of a slender tail, the creature vanished, leaving behind only ripples. The ripples diminished while expanding until the surface became calm again. Looking like a large, moving and menacing stick, a water snake slithered across the river.

Having relieved some aches in the numbing cold water, Seth got back into his canoe. Cougar had waited patiently in the bow. Seth paddled downstream, turning toward the bank in front of the first cabin at Foxwood.

TEN

HUNT CABIN

Sethrum turned on the single light hanging from the ceiling of his cabin. He felt weary as well as angry although food seemed to be the first requirement. Working quickly, he prepared a stew for himself and Cougar. A fire was soon blazing in the wood stove, drying air in the building along with providing heat. Together with a fine fragrance of smoke, there mingled aromas of simmering beef, onions, carrots, tomatoes, potatoes and celery.

Cougar was served first. After a large meal of stew, he stretched out and slept on his bear rug at the foot of Seth's cot. Near this bed, next to the trunk, Seth sat in his favorite chair and enjoyed mixed flavors of stew served in a bowl and followed by the usual coffee. While sipping coffee slowly, he thought, I'll first check my ownership of this resort then push forward all development plans. Full speed ahead is the way to proceed now. I like to work and build things. I won't be surrendering to a gang like the Wild Society. Possession of the old, hunt cabin means everything because that site is the center for development. If lawyers can't get that gang out of my cabin, I'll just move in there myself.

For the next few days, Seth went back to his usual work of painting almost everything in addition to cleaning windows, putting on screens, staining docks, varnishing cedar strip boats, cutting grass and splitting firewood. Business plans took shape rapidly. Seth obtained ownership of Foxwood with an area of land that included the old, hunt cabin. Sufficient partners were obtained to establish the Fox Condominium Company. Although Seth did most of the actual work, Phil Dobbs became president of the Company. Seth kept the resort separate from the Company. At a later time, the Company could expand to take over the resort. Phil and Katherine Dobbs managed the resort for Seth. They also continued to live at the resort's house and office.

Seth led the Company's attack against the Wild Society. Lawyers from both sides worked on legal aspects of the conflict. People have to abide by the law, Seth told himself as he sipped coffee in his cabin. We have to work within the law although it often seems unjust and on the side of the best lawyers. I must not have the best lawyers in this case because the Society still occupies the hunt cabin. They paid Phil and Katherine for the use of the place. We can't start anything until we control the site.

Sethrum poured fresh coffee into his cup then returned to his chair to formulate a plan. We must all work under the rule of law, he said to himself, even if justice seems to get bent in favor of one group or another. Even a bent justice is better than a criminal system. Law is our protection from a breakdown in social order. However, I should give the legal system a little push to try to get the process to be more on my side. I'll simply visit my hunt cabin. If I leave everything to lawyers nothing will happen. I'm going to have to make something happen. I would like to detect some progress. I guess I'll have to stir things a little because I'm tired of waiting.

Accompanied by Cougar, Sethrum packed his usual traveling equipment and placed everything in the canoe. Suddenly feeling a sense of urgency, he paddled up the Fox River. Tree pollen drifted like yellow dust in the wind and coated the water. A chattering group of grackles pestered a nest-raiding crow. A fox, the color of pollen, stood at the water's edge. The animal stared at the canoe briefly before picking up a fish, climbing the bank and slipping out of view amid a thicket of brush. One vulture watched from the top of a stump while a second scavenger pulled entrails from a dead sucker. Glossy, black wings brushed against cool air as two ravens flew across the sky. Mergansers moved away from the canoe's path. The craft left a gradually diminishing trail of ripples along the calm river. When bleached logs of the hunt cabin could be seen among the trees, the canoe's bow turned toward the bank. Seth paddled to the sandy shoreline. Cougar jumped from the bow. Seth stepped into shallow water and pulled his craft only a little onto the sand. He left his canoe at the water's edge so he could leave in an hurry if he got into trouble.

Carrying his rifle, and with Cougar by his side, Sethrum approached the building. The dog showed no sign of concern. No one seemed to be present although two canoes were hidden in brush. This is the site of my new complex, Seth said to himself. But nothing can be done until I get the Society out of here.

Seth proceeded to the front door and opened it. He and Cougar went inside the building. Entering with them, drifted currents of air laced with a fine perfume from wild, apple blossoms. Ashes in the fireplace were cold. Nothing stirred to disturb an eerie stillness. The unnatural silence indicated a recent—almost lingering—presence of people although no one seemed to be in the house. Cougar and Seth checked the place slowly.

Sleeping bags were stretched out neatly on some of the bunks. The kitchen was clean. The sink's counter shone. A fragrance of soap wafted in the air. I must give them credit for keeping a neat camp, observed Seth. This cabin will have to be removed to make way for our new buildings. I'll be sorry to see this place go.

Metallic, squeaking sounds, like those caused by a vehicle's breaks, came from the parking area behind the building. Cougar growled. A shiver ran through Seth. Looking out a back window, he saw five people getting out of a red van. Taisse Cantry and Sal Perkins led this group to the back door. Behind them, walked the large man and two other men who had been present the previous night.

Using a rope to serve as a leash, Seth hastily tied Cougar to a kitchen chair then got his rifle before he opened the door. Filling the doorway, he stated, "The owner's here now."

The group halted. Sal paled somewhat. Her mouth opened as she and the others stared at the doorway and the man with a gun.

The large man recovered quickly from the initial shock. Angry now, he pushed ahead of the group. His hulking form loomed largely toward the doorway.

Leaning his rifle against the wall, Seth gripped the upper doorframe with both of his hands. He lifted himself up off the floor and kicked sharply, sinking a boot into the man's midsection. He doubled over and fell in a gasping, contorted pile. He forced himself to recover swiftly, caught his breath and looked up just before a boot lodged itself against his face and shot forward sending him backward, knocking over the two other men.

They rallied in fury. Two men ran to the front of the cabin. The big man, like an angry bull, approached the doorway. He moved slowly, certain of his strength, although this time he would be more careful.

Seth heard the front door being opened. Boots tapped against the floor. Two men were rushing toward him. He turned around in time to avoid being knocked over by the onrush. Seth grabbed the closest attacker and continued his charge directly at the large man, sending them both tumbling outside.

A blood-curdling shriek came from behind Seth. He swung around and saw Cougar's jaws clamped next to a man's crotch. His face ashen, he screamed again. Seth picked up his gun, pointed it toward the doorway and pulled on the back of Cougar's neck. The dog released his grip. The terrified man grabbed his crotch and moved outside. To people near the door, he said, "That dog's crazy." Walking to the far side of the van, the fellow delayed to check his injury. Next he got into the vehicle and drove away quickly, leaving behind a swirl of exhaust fumes along with some laughter.

The two remaining men along with the women approached the back door. The large fellow was the first to enter the building. Checking the rooms quickly, he discovered that the intruders had left and were in the canoe.

With Cougar in the bow, Seth paddled back toward his cabin. I needed some action, he explained to himself. I can't keep waiting for someone to do something—especially when I think nothing is being done. One way or another, I'm going to keep up the attack until the Society people leave so I can develop this area. Maybe before the flies get any worse, I'll explore the Indian trail. A lot has happened along that route.

To Cougar, Seth said, "You're a good dog." Hearing those familiar and welcome words, Cougar seemed to smile or, at least, looked pleased. "You're not a mean dog," added Seth. "You certainly know, however, how to defend yourself and me. You also know a few good holds. Tomorrow we'll travel along the trail."

When the canoe reached the bank in front of the cabin, Cougar jumped from the bow. Seth stepped out of his craft. He concealed it among bushes then followed Cougar to the cabin. Inside the practical yet comfortable home, Seth immediately started preparing his equipment for a walking trip along the trail. An evening sky was tinted by purple light from the setting sun by the time Seth finished his work. The sun, obscured by a purple haze, turned scarlet before fading into a pink glow along the horizon.

Cougar slept on his bearskin rug while Seth rested in his chair next to the cot. During my fishing trip to the south, he reflected, I saw great country as well as people. I enjoyed fine accommodation. At the same time, I saw a beautiful environment where there was also wilderness. I'm going to develop this river so tourists can enjoy it with the best accommodations. The Society can find another wild spot to protect.

Other places have original beauty. This area has nothing unique that I can see. One forest is the same as another. Developing another, wild site won't do any harm.

Sitting in his chair, accompanied by his thoughts, Seth went to sleep. He was awakened by a melody of robins' songs. He collected his traveling equipment and stepped outside with Cougar. They followed the road behind Foxwood then turned off at a lane leading north.

The gray light of dawn filtered through the forest, clarifying the forms of trees beside the winding route. Robins continued to sing. This melody rang clearly through misty air. Robins welcome the start of each new day just as people should, observed Seth.

The first side road, jutting away from the main route, led to the hunt cabin. This road was marked by fresh tire prints. A fragrance of wood smoke drifted with air currents. A van was parked behind the building.

Beyond the cabin's turnoff, the trail ceased to be a usable road after dipping into an hollow which was crossed by a stream. Only specialized vehicles could proceed beyond this point, noted Sethrum.

After cutting through an open area of rippling grass, the rutted lane turned up an hill and passed over smooth rocks bordered by white pines. The elevated section dropped to a creek that splashed under a dilapidated, log bridge. After leaving this bridge, the path topped out on smooth rocks. The rocks provided a view westward to a series of beaver ponds held in place by extensive dams.

Seth proceeded to a rocky promontory jutting out toward the ponds. Close to this stretch of rock, there was a beaver lodge littered with freshly chewed poplar branches.

Using pieces of dry hardwood, Sethrum kindled a fire to prepare breakfast. He fried potatoes and eggs before perking coffee. Cougar chewed on cooked meat and dog biscuits. While both dog and man enjoyed a meal, sunlight shot through openings in foliage and shone on ripples formed by two beavers swimming on the closest pond. They came over to investigate the visitors then slipped under the water's rippled surface.

Seth found a section of eroded rock where he could lie down comfortably. He used his traveling pack as a cushion.

Having enjoyed a short rest, he kindled a fire in order to perk coffee. He sat on the rocks and drank coffee while he watched sunlight dancing on the pond. Black spruce bordered the water. Higher terrain was topped by white pines. An errant breeze occasionally whispered passed pine boughs and ruffled the ponds. Sunlight edged with gold the strands of cloud drifting across an azure sky. Caught by the beauty of the landscape, Seth allowed himself to rest. His fatigue gradually eased and he slept on the rock warmed by sunlight. When the vision happened, he knew he was starting the events foreseen by Sihoki.

ELEVEN

THE VISION

Cougar continued to sleep beside the campfire. Sethrum walked back to the trail. He found a footpath leading north. He proceeded cautiously. On each side, lofty pines reached above dense foliage. A shrill cry of an eagle pierced a light layer of clouds.

Seeing a large rattlesnake sunning itself on a sandy section of pathway, Seth left the trail and returned to it as it crossed flat rocks before entering a low area where moose as well as deer tracks marked soft earth.

Intrigued by the network of tracks, Seth watched them more closely, detecting prints of a variety of animals including bears, wolves, lynxes, foxes and cougars. The sky darkened with what became a passing cloud of birds. Passenger pigeons, Seth said to himself. I'm either in a remotely wild place overlooked by the ravages of time or, in some way, I've gone back in time. My surroundings look the way they must have been over an hundred years ago. Maybe I'm at the well-recorded year of 1720. I don't know how this has occurred; yet I can see these things. Strangely, I don't fear what's happening. However, I must be cautious. I don't know what has started. I'm in more than a dream. I'm not dreaming that I'm here. I'm really here.

On air currents drifting from the north, Seth detected a fragrance of wood smoke mixed with aromas of roasting fowl. Someone's doing a lot of cooking farther up the trail, Seth said to himself. I'll have to be careful in this place.

He stopped when he thought he heard the sounds of a person snoring. The sounds came from the wide base of a white pine's trunk. Here a man was sitting with his back resting against the trunk and his head was tilted down. He was sleeping and snored occasionally. Seth stared at the man who wore a bearskin cloak over a deerskin jacket. His breechcloth, leggings and moccasins were also made of deer hide. One eagle feather was tied to his long, black hair. A bow and quiver of arrows were secured to his back while a leather belt held a knife and tomahawk. A spear had dropped from his hand. Maybe he's from one of the Algonkian nations, thought Seth as he turned away and started hurrying northward along the trail.

A whizzing sound came from trees ahead before an arrow slammed into a pine trunk beside Seth, kicking bark chips onto his face. He crouched, just missing a second arrow coming from the same direction and hissing passed the trunk. This might be a vision but I could get killed here, he told himself, sensing his fear and knowing he was sweating.

When a spear came from behind him and whooshed over his head, he ran north with all his strength. By the pounding sounds on his back trail, he knew he was being pursued. All his senses awakened in a way he had not known before. His nerves tightened with fear although he did not panic. He kept thinking while his heart pounded and he ran with all the strength he could muster.

During his wild dash forward, he concentrated on not losing the trail. It wound upward until reaching the top of an hill overlooking a beaver pond. On the pond's far shore, an army was encamped. Numerous, small cooking fires sent out traces of smoke laced with a sweet, oily aroma of roasting meat. French and Algonkians, Seth told himself. They must be cooking passenger pigeons.

He continued running. Rushing at full speed down a steep grade, he was partly stumbling and falling when he saw the two French soldiers. Unable to check his momentum, he threw himself forward with extra force, colliding with the soldiers and sending them sprawling into brush beside the path. They yelled before two shots splintered branches above Seth's head. He dropped to a lower part of the path and splashed through shallow water.

He ran until he was wet with sweat. Fatigue pulled at him then dissolved with an infusion of a dwindling remnant of strength. His heart seemed to be pounding so loudly his enemies could hear it.

Sounds of pursuit vanished after the shots had been fired. To listen more carefully, in addition to getting some rest, he stepped into dense brush beside the trail. In a short time, he heard branches being rustled farther ahead. These sounds grew louder until two

Algonkian hunters walked passed. Each carried a deer.

The hunters moved quickly out of view. Seth rejoined the path. Again he ran north until exhaustion forced him to continue more slowly.

When the route led up an hill crested by pines, he threw himself down among exposed roots of a white pine. From this position, he could watch his back trail. Although fatigue had washed over him, he could not sleep. He watched a pale sky where a gentle breeze moved strands of a cloud in to a formation resembling an eagle's head. The forest is endlessly beautiful and interesting, reflected Seth. Yet people are at war here. I have to warn the Mohawk village that an army is going to attack.

The need to warn the village sent an extra flow of energy pulsing into Seth's weary muscles. He got up and started running at a steady pace he hoped he could maintain. He ran for a long time until all he knew was running. There was ahead always the path winding among a moving panorama of large trunks and dense foliage.

Gradually the route came to more open areas leading to a vast extent of cultivated fields. Stretching westward, there was the sparkling water of Spirit Lake. Sethrun had also accumulated four armed guards. Two men ran in front of him and two followed.

Seth noticed women hoeing in the fields. A palisade of poles surrounded the village. The two leading guards ran through an opening in the palisade. Seth followed and was accompanied by the other two men. A number of bark-covered longhouses filled the interior of the village. Men, women and children gathered to see the visitor. Smoke drifted away from openings at the top of longhouses. Dogs followed a group of people who led Seth inside a longhouse.

Smoke from central fires curled lazily across shafts of light dropping through openings in the ceiling. These lights revealed a long, narrow building with sleeping, or resting, and storage platforms along each side. Braided ears of corn in addition to spices hung from the ceiling. Pottery pots were common household items as were wooden, splint baskets.

Some of the women and children continued cooking, sewing or tending fires. Others sat on platforms. A few people greeted visitors until a large crowd filled the structure.

A man who approached Seth had white hair. His medium length hair protruded from under a deer antler headdress containing three, eagle feathers. His clothing was made of deerskin. Speaking English softly, he asked, "You're an English trader?"

"Yes," replied Seth, thinking of no better answer.

"Who travels with you?" asked this man who was obviously a chief.

"Ridgeworth Moon," Seth replied. "I'm Sethrum Moon. Does everyone here speak English?"

"Some do," answered the chief. His face was lined. His tan-colored eyes were alert. He acted calmly as if he had seen most things before.

Wanting to be direct because he was tired, Sethrum said, "I came to warn you that an army is going to attack this village." Pointing southward, he continued to say, "The army is coming along that trail. I think they are Algonkians and French. I saw them camped beside a large beaver pond on an hill."

People moved quickly. Most left the building and Seth followed them. He couldn't understand what the people were saying. They were, however, organized and soon runners ran ahead down the trail, followed by a swiftly moving army of men.

Although Seth was weary, he did his best to keep up with the others. When they reached the vicinity of the beaver pond, large groups stayed behind and moved into the woods on each side. A small force continued down the central trail. Seth stayed with the center group. A large fellow handed him a war club. He was surprised to see so many men being quickly deployed and moving quietly without confusion. Catching a glimpse of the white haired man talking to someone up ahead, Seth said to himself, I must try to keep him in sight because he speaks English.

A time of waiting followed. Voices could be heard in the enemy camp. Occasionally someone shouted or laughed. Otherwise the forest was unusually quiet except for distant calls of ravens. Far above, an eagle screamed. Close to Seth, a blue jay started shrieking. Its last shrieking sound was cut in half, likely because the bird was shot with an arrow to stop this call of alarm from ringing through the woods. A silence returned that was unnerving.

Resonant, piercing, war cries cut through the forest as a wave of running men agilely flowed away from the concealment of trees and attacked the camp. This first thrust into the enemy position was a furious assault. It caught the French and Algonkians completely by surprise. They were almost routed.

The army fell back, regrouped and started to put up resistance. Seth became worried when he saw the Mohawks start to falter. Losing their orderliness, they moved back the way they had come until they were in full retreat, being pursued by a rapidly advancing and greatly outnumbering force.

Seth saw the white haired man fall with an arrow in his leg. He got up again, turned around and held a war club in readiness for attackers charging toward him as well as around him.

Admiring the man's courage, Seth took a position beside him. Together they struck out at onrushing foes. Continuously, the enemies kept coming. The forest became a din of shouts, screams and shots. Arrows, spears and tomahawks flashed more silently. A sweet smell of blood mixed with odors of sweat and acrid, gun smoke.

Many soldiers, astonished to be faced by two enemies, continued to rush passed on either side. They went by like water flowing around two rocks in a stream. Those that did not move aside had to be fought with war club or knife. Fallen foes, like driftwood caught on snags, helped turn aside the charging force.

After most of the army had gone passed, the white haired man said to Seth, "They're in the trap now. They'll be attacked up ahead and will retreat back this way." After the man had spoken, there erupted, to the north, a furious outburst of shooting. Following the first blasts, shots became more sporadic.

Mohawks took positions on each side of Seth and the chief, getting ready for a second ambush. When beleaguered remnants of the retreating army appeared, a ragged volley of shots brought down more of the enemies. Arrows whizzed through the air followed by an orderly onrush of men toward the shambles of the army. The flow of battle broke quickly into a dwindling number of skirmishes until the struggle was over. Those who could retreat melted quickly into the forest. The white haired man turned to Seth and said, "You've warned our village. You fought beside me. You will have the name, Red Wolf. I am called Tall Pine. In order to join this battle, I had to remove my title of chief. I will take it up again when we get back to the village."

"Thanks for the name," replied Seth. "I like it. I've never before acquired so many enemies at one time. At such a

Pelican Moon

time, I appreciate a friend. I like the way you plan a battle."

"Many have a voice in planning such a battle," replied Tall Pine. "We will return to our village."

Because of Tall Pine's leg injury and Seth's fatigue, the two men walked slowly along the trail leading to the village. In the village, Seth became quickly known as Red Wolf, the one who had warned the village and helped Tall Pine in the battle. Seth was also seen as an English trader working with his relative, Ridgeworth Moon. Seth was often called Wolf Moon.

At the village, Seth noted the fields prepared for planting. The palisade enclosed the place where the river came out of the ground. Tall trees bordered the lake.

In the community, there seemed to be constant activity. Men worked to prepare the land. Many old stumps were being removed, although not all of them. Women did the planting and would tend the crops in addition to looking after their families. Some women fished, as did the men. Most of the potters were women although men often made their own pipes. Men hunted for fresh meat.

Inside the longhouse, Sethrum sat at the side of a fire used by Tall Pine's family. His wife, Planter, was a slim woman. Gray hair bordered her finely chiseled face where brown eyes observed her home with kindness and sensitivity. She was in charge of her immediate family as well as the rest of the longhouse. Planter and Tall Pine had two, married sons who were away living in their wives' families' longhouses. Two, married daughters lived in Planter's longhouse. "Family life is organized by the women," Tall Pine said to Seth. "The head of a longhouse family is the clan mother, such as Planter. She selects a chief who becomes a clan representative in our village council. Chiefs from this village take part in a council for the

Mohawk nation which sends chiefs to a council for the Confederacy in the land of the Onondagas."

Using one side of a fire in the dwelling, there was Planter, Tall Pine and one, unmarried daughter called Corn Tassel. "The way women have life organized will become clearer to you in time," Planter told Seth. She kept her hair tied away from her face with a deer hide strip. When she smiled, lines deepened at the sides of her mouth and eyes. She was a good worker, providing well for her family. "Women select the chiefs," explained Planter. "If they don't do what we think they should be doing, we can remove them and select new chiefs."

Tall Pine's resonant voice made him a good speaker. He spoke in an unhurried way and he was an interesting storyteller. "Men look after the councils," said Tall Pine. "We clear the fields so the women can grow crops. We defend the village. We have trading to do as well as hunting and the building of things like longhouses."

"You and your family and many other people here speak English along with Mohawk," said Seth to Tall Pine. "How did so many people come to speak English?"

"We trade with the English," answered Tall Pine. "They come to our councils. We go to their councils. We help the English to organize their councils. We were asked how we run our Confederacy so we helped those people to run their Confederacy. We also help each other fight our enemies."

A frequent meal Seth received was corn soup along with corn bread. Tantalizing aromas of cooking food mixed with fragrances of wood smoke and sweet grass. Herbs and spices added scents from the ceiling where these plants were dried in addition to an abundant supply of corn. Ears of corn were braided together and hung from the ceiling.

Inside the longhouse, there was a flowing stream of human life. This society was active and always interesting. Seth enjoyed sitting beside the fire and talking to people. Individuals who could speak English visited him.

Large events took place in the center of the village. During dances, people would move in circles and lines flowing to the beat of drums and rattles that accompanied the singing.

Sethrum liked to visit people who were working in the fields. Children dressed similarly to their parents and often worked with them. Young children stayed with their mothers. Adults, children or dogs usually accompanied Seth during his walks throughout the village.

Hunters brought in game of all sorts from turkeys and passenger pigeons to deer, moose or bears. Wildlife was abundant. The river, lake and forest combined to form a vast storehouse where the villagers' skills enabled them to obtain fine provisions.

One day, while Sethrum and Tall Pine were sitting beside the fire, the chief said, "Our crops are everything to us. When the corn, beans and squash harvest becomes too small, we move our village to a different place. We nourish the earth in our fields with fish and ashes. We try to move crops as much as possible. Although we help the earth, we eventually change locations. This also helps us get a better supply of firewood. We're clearing land south of here, getting ready for our next village. It will be located more in our territory. Before we go, we will have new fields cleared and planted so we won't miss a growing season."

"How far south have you traveled?" asked Seth.

"I've been to the English villages and the salt water," answered Tall Pine. "I've also been to the salt water farther south. During my last trip, far to the south, I took Planter as well as Corn Tassel."

Planter finished adding wood to the fire. She sat down and, with a smile flashing across her face, she said, "Actually Corn Tassel and I took Tall Pine and others south. I've been there before. The salt water, in that direction, is a long way away. There are trails to take by water and land. We traveled over the mountains and down through the territory of the Susquehanna. By passing along mountains toward the setting sun, we visited the Cherokee. I like the mountains. Our camp was higher than the clouds. They drifted below us and sometimes around us. Ravens and crows flew beside or below us. The eagles stayed above. There were large rattlesnakes around and many deer.

After leaving the mountains, we traveled south to flat land. We kept going until we camped beside salt water. We stayed on a strip of land, likely an island. There were a lot o' snakes in that country and large turtles. We saw many different animals, birds, fish and plants. Some were not different such as deer, bears and cougars.

We met Seminoles. One of them was a Tocobaga woman who did shell work. With her, I traded flint arrowheads for a shell necklace. I gave it to my daughter, Corn Tassel.

I liked to watch the pelicans. I carved a pelican design on a piece of bone and put this mark on my pottery. I use this pelican design on all my pottery work. A lot of people don't notice the pelican symbol within the circular, bone print in the pottery. However, the pelican moon is always there. I gave a pelican designed, deer antler to the Tocobaga woman. She started using this mark on her pottery. Maybe I started a new design in the south."

Planter stopped talking and prepared a type of coffee made from a charred cob

Pelican Moon

of corn. She served this drink along with corn bread before she continued to say, "The Seminoles fought the Spanish and English to protect that beautiful land. The Tocobaga, like the others, fought the Spanish who were invaders seeking gold. They killed people in order to take their gold as well as their land. The Spanish destroyed villages to get gold."

Seth enjoyed the coffee-like drink. Cornbread was tasty. He became accustomed to soft sounding voices telling stories. He particularly enjoyed listening to Planter and Tall Pine. Seth was absorbed in one story, picturing the events in his mind, when Planter suddenly stopped talking and turned her sparkling gaze directly at him, sending a shiver coursing through him. He felt that something serious was about to happen. "Wolf Moon," she said, shooting the words through him, making his heart pound faster. "We thank you for helping us. This land also needs your help. Always protect this land. Do not misunderstand me, Wolf Moon. We don't worship the land or its parts. We worship only the Creator. But the Creator made the land so we must respect his works and wishes. The land is a work of the Creator and continues to be part of the Creator. Always treat the earth respectfully. Sure we have to have places for fields and villages. However, we must never take more than we need or take wastefully. There's much to be learned about the Creator and his works. There lingers, in every pine needle, a touch of God's presence. There's nothing but God; so we must not destroy any part. In the beauty of even a pine needle, or a bird's feather, we can begin to appreciate the Holder of the Heavens. Doing the Creator's will brings us closer to the Great Spirit and our own happiness. Going against the Creator's will takes us away to unhappiness. I think we should choose to experience life happily. The land is the Creator's property. We must never use such gifts unwisely. Don't presume you can do better. There's a spiritual presence of God in life and that is the real gold."

Planter served more of the dark, corn drink, then she said, "The missionaries visited us at our last village. Much of their message, we found that we already knew. We could see, however, that they carried a message we, like others, required when they said people who believed in Christ were helped to return to God. Such people could find their way back to God and, as a result, experience personal happiness. Christ shows us a path to God. If we take this path and get closer to the Creator, we experience life happily, rather than remain farther away and experience life unhappily. All human beings are helped by such a message. We also need our own ways.

We respect this earth. If you need something from the land, use only what is needed. While you are getting what you need, don't destroy the land because a destroyed land will give you nothing. We can't make the Creator's work more beautiful. We need trails, homes and food. Yet if we don't really require something, don't take it and never ruin what God has made."

"And you thought I was a talker," said Tall Pine to Seth.

"Maybe I've talked enough for now," replied Planter.

Seth left the longhouse and stepped outside into cold air. A group of children ran passed him. Adults spoke to him. He walked passed two men who were playing a wagering game using flat, rounded pieces of pottery. A woman scraped a bear hide. Freshly caught fish were being smoked on racks.

The palisade around the village enclosed the place where the river emerged from the ground. From here, the water flowed out from openings between poles in the palisade. Continuing

Pelican Moon

onward, this stream joined the lake before moving southward again as a river.

North, along the lake's shore, gray patches revealed stretches of rock topped by stately pines. The south shoreline was flatter although densely treed. The village, with its fields, occupied much of the east shore.

Sethrum enjoyed the company of Corn Tassel. She was slim and of medium height. Her eyes were almond brown. She kept her long, black hair tied away from her face by means of a deerskin cord. She had an unobtrusive beauty. From her mother, Corn Tassel had learned the art of working with pottery and, like her mother, Tassel used the pelican moon design on all her pieces of pottery. Unlike Planter, Tassel, applied a pair of the pelican, bone impressions. She always used the double pelican symbol even on pipes.

Clay from the river was of fine quality requiring the addition of very little crushed stone to make strong pottery. Planter and Tassel spent most of their time making bowls and pipes. These items were prized in the village and used for trade. Aside from her pottery, Tassel's most prized possession was the shell necklace her mother had obtained by trading with the Tocobaga woman in the south. Tassel always wore this necklace. As often as possible, she and her mother worked at pottery outside their longhouse while the commotion of village life swirled around them.

Birds' songs drifted into the village from the surrounding forest. Robins sang at dusk or dawn. A call of an ovenbird could be heard much of the day. Loons cried from the lake. Whippoorwills were numerous. Their clear calls rang through the village at night. Eagles soared overhead and nested in dead, white pines north of the village. Ravens frolicked throughout the area.

Animals were abundant. Men trapped beavers for trade with Ridgeworth Moon. Deer were plentiful, as were moose. Seth saw a cougar on the north side of the lake. Most other fur bearing animals were present such as the fisher, mink, otter, weasel and lynx. Bears, wolves, foxes and rabbits were common. Most types of birds were plentiful, particularly ducks and geese.

"We need trails, villages and food," said Planter one misty morning while she worked at pottery with Tassel in front of their longhouse. "We prepare fields for crops and work to increase harvests. However, whenever possible, the land is best when it is left untouched by people. To be sure we don't ruin what the Creator has made in land or water, we must not tamper unnecessarily with such original work. We don't worship the forest. We worship only God whose majesty and presence can be seen or at least partially glimpsed in his works. All things are aspects of God. We are all parts of the whole Creator who experiences life through all these separate, yet connected, parts. We live forever; therefore time has no relevance in the spirit world where we can travel from present to past or future and back again. We can begin to imagine the limitless grandeur of the mind of God in viewing an area such as this lake with its river running through the forest. The lake teems with life and reflects the sky. Clouds drift above the water and move in reflections on the surface. The shore has good soil along with rocky hills and the tallest trees. Maybe other areas are less important. This is a special place used for visions. Enjoy the river as it is. Don't alter this particular site. We must use the earth with respect."

Seth found himself increasingly attracted to Corn Tassel. She often accompanied Seth and Tall Pine or Planter during trips to get fish, plants

Pelican Moon

or game. Marriage plans were made for Wolf Moon and Corn Tassel.

TWELVE

THE GULF

Sethrum heard barking. The barking was distant, but got louder until he realized Cougar was standing very close and barking persistently. "What's wrong with you?" asked Seth as the dog started whining loudly. "It's all right," said Seth. "I had a vision that Sihoki told me about."

Seth stood up, looked around and noticed that the trees were smaller. The trail had two, rutted lanes instead of one path. "Let's go home," said Seth to the dog whereby they both started walking back down the Indian trail. They passed the hunt cabin. A van was parked at the back. Smoke drifted lazily from the chimney. Seth and Cougar proceeded to their own cabin.

This place looks familiar and good, thought Seth after he switched on the light hanging from the ceiling. Next he crumpled some paper, put it in the stove and added kindling plus three large pieces of wood before striking a match to start the fire. He closed the door, checked the draft and listened to an increasingly loud throbbing of flames. A slight fragrance of wood smoke seeped into the air.

Seth opened cans to get beans for himself in addition to meaty, dog food for Cougar. After eating the food and drinking water from his bowl, Cougar stretched out on his bear rug and was soon asleep. Seth enjoyed his favorite meal of beans and crackers. Next he perked coffee. While waiting for the coffee, he checked his equipment. He filled his cup with fragrant, steaming coffee and sat in the comfortable chair next to his cot. Looking out the front window at sunlight illuminating foliage, he thought, I told Sihoki I would let Cougar try racing. I will have to take him to Will. I also have to tell Sihoki about what happened to me on the Indian trail.

Sethrum hastily prepared his equipment. When everything was ready, he opened the front, passenger door so Cougar could jump inside to his place on the passenger seat. After closing this door, Seth walked around to the driver's side, opened the door, got inside and started the truck. It lurched out of the driveway and turned onto the road.

He stopped at a restaurant to get a take-out cup of coffee. For Cougar, he got a cup of water. After arranging cassettes of music, Seth started driving southward.

Highways led through a landscape of verdant foliage. The sun's color deepened from pink to purple while descending into clouds along the horizon. Much later, crimson light from

Pelican Moon

the moon shot through the night. Crimson hues drained away from the moon as it ascended from an haze along the horizon.

During the trip, the emerald green of wilderness became increasingly laced by an infusion of gray from cities and highways. Sethrum enjoyed the routes of the highways as they wound through vistas of fields, rivers, lakes, forests and cities. Eventually he reached the trail leading to the village on the mountaintop in the Smoky Mountains. While following this trail, Seth looked for, but found no sign of, the old cougar, Flop Ear.

One of Sethrum's camping places was on a level area below the mountaintop. Oaks and hemlocks dripped with moisture from drifting clouds. They floated in endless, white layers pierced by veiled peaks. Strands of upward drifting vapor turned to gold when touched by sunlight. Through breaks in this cover, blue valleys appeared where sunlight glimmered on roofs or sides of houses. Miniature buildings dotted a pastel colored quilt of fields. Crows and ravens called. An eagle screamed from misty heights.

Mist brushed through camp while Seth added wood to a tall fire. He perked coffee then fried some onions in a pan before roasting steaks for himself and Cougar. Having filled his cup with coffee, Seth sat down to watch distant peaks above a valley veiled by a blue haze.

Seth and Cougar continued walking until they reached the mountaintop village where they were welcomed into the home of Will Panther. Seth sat on a chair at the western side of a blazing fireplace. Cougar sat next to him. After bringing the dog water in a bowl and giving Seth coffee, Will refilled his cup with coffee before sitting on a chair at the other side of the fire. "You've taken good care of Cougar," said Will who was obviously pleased with the condition of the dog. "He looks strong."

"He's traveled a long way since he was here before," replied Seth. "I told Sihoki I would bring Cougar back for racing at least once."

"I've trained Cougar to race," said Will. "He's a natural runner and I really didn't have to do much with him. I think Hog Hunter did most of the training."

"Where's Hog Hunter now?" asked Seth.

"We retired him," answered Will. "He was here with me and left for a longer time than usual. He was sick when he got back. The cougar hung around outside 'til Hunter died. We think a rattler bit him. Hunter hated snakes. Afterward the cougar left and that's the last time I've seen her."

"I'm sorry to hear about Hog Hunter," said Sethrum. "As I mentioned, I told Sihoki I would let Cougar have a chance to race. I should get traveling because

I'll take Cougar to Sihoki then I have to get back to work up north."

Both men looked through the window as sunlight emblazoned rising tendrils of vapor. "Sihoki told me I was on a spiritual journey," said Seth. "When I was up north, on an old, Indian trail, I had a vision of the past. I went back through time over two hundred years."

"My sister told me you were heading toward an experience with the spirit world," said Will. "She can see things."

Will served corn bread in addition to more coffee. He gave Cougar a large biscuit. Sitting down again, Will said, "During the time period you visited in your vision, all the Indian hunters could not diminish the supplies of the wilderness. Today, there is less and less of the natural garden. At the present time, the Indian hunters alone could clear out the provisions in the forest. We now have to harvest our natural garden with enormous care. Uses of land, water and air have to be closely regulated."

"I've been learning much about the environment lately," replied Seth before he stood up. Seth's action stirred Cougar. The dog stood and stretched then walked slowly toward the door. "Thanks for your hospitality; but I should get Cougar back to Sihoki."

Will walked with Seth and they both placed their cups in the kitchen sink. "Thanks for the coffee and bread," said Seth.

"In a day or two," replied Will. "I'll go down and make sure Cougar's ready for a race. You should take him to Sihoki because my sister wants to see you."

"I'll get started," said Seth. He opened the door. Cougar went outside first and was followed by Seth and Will. "Please let me know when Cougar will be racing," said Seth. "I'd like to see his first race."

"Okay," said Will. "You'll be hearing from me."

"Thanks," replied Seth. "I'll be seeing you." Seth walked toward the dog and drifting strands of mist enveloped them.

Although visibility was reduced by the vapor, Seth was able to follow Cougar along the trail. An eagle screamed from a narrow patch of blue sky. Hooves could be heard tapping against the ground as deer bounded away from the path. Cougar killed a rattlesnake that was too slow in getting out of the way. After stopping twice to camp, the two travelers reached the truck and continued their journey southward. They drove across a land where crops stirred in warming sunlight. Alligators rested in shallow pools or along clay banks beside some roads. Seth also saw a bear and an eagle along with a few vultures and turkeys.

Morning air was hot and humid when Sethrum knocked on the door of Sihoki's home next to the river. She came to the door, carrying a tray containing coffee for herself and Seth in addition to water for Cougar. There was also some corn bread. "You were expecting company?" asked Seth as he held the door for her.

"Yes," she answered before proceeding to a table next to two chairs located in the shade of the live oak. Sihoki and Seth sat down and rested while sipping coffee. Mockingbirds sang almost continuously. Seth talked about bringing Cougar back for racing and the experiences along the Indian trail.

"Thanks for bringing Cougar here for a series of races," she said. "He's a natural champion if he wants to be one. Some dogs don't take to racing. Some do. I'll make sure you know when he's racing."

As her eyes sparkled, Sihoki said, "Sethrum Moon, you've come a long way and learned a lot since a shark brought you here."

"Yes, I've had quite a fishing trip," he answered while admiring the woman's face. It was lined with kindness and wisdom. Her wealth is her knowledge, he told himself. I wish she would more directly tell me what she knows and is thinking.

"Seth," said Sihoki, "we once had a small number of hunters and much game. Now we have a small amount of game and many hunters. Today, hunters must be closely regulated. We once had a small number of buildings and great expanses of wilderness. Now we have small amounts of wilderness and many buildings. The remaining wilderness must be strictly protected. You received a vision showing you the past so you can see your future. Visions reveal to us that in the spirit world there aren't the same restrictions that restrict humans here on earth."

She stopped talking to listen to a melodious combination of bird songs coming from the swamp. "You are a good listener, Seth," observed Sihoki. "Each situation can have a good message for us if we are watching as well as listening and, sometimes, looking back."

Standing up, she said, "I'm going to get more coffee. Do you want some more?"

"No, but thanks," answered Seth. "I've some traveling to do. I don't like to leave without that dog."

"Almost as soon as you arrived, he went out to check his old trails," said Sihoki. "After he has had a chance to try a real race, at least once, you can have him back."

"Thanks," replied Seth. "I'll look forward to hearing about the mutt."

"That's some mutt," she said with a smile. "I'll let you know."

"Thanks for the coffee and bread," said Seth before he turned to start walking to his truck. He got into his vehicle and drove to the highway. He drove slowly in order to enjoy the surrounding beauty along the way to the Blue Heron Motel.

At the motel, life continued in its timeless way. After leaving the chimney, the heron flew to the beach in front of Seth's balcony where the egret waited. Both received some fish and shrimp purchased at a bait shop. Always looking for fish, pelicans swooped over the waves. Backs of dolphins splashed through the surface periodically. Sandpipers checked the shoreline where waves crashed along the sand and rushed back to the sea.

Deciding to do some shelling, Seth waded into the water then walked parallel to the beach. Stingrays slithered out of his way. Scaled sardines along with some glass minnows circled him. Mullet swam passed through deeper, greenish-blue water.

Seth walked slowly, watching the creatures. A shark's fin broke through the surface of the water close to Seth. This fin cut through the surface in circling movements before dipping out of view. Seth noted the presence of welk shells along with fighting conchs, sea urchins and starfish.

In a particularly large wave that was rising upward and cresting while approaching him, Seth saw a school of mullet. Sunlight illuminated the fish while adding gold to the greenish water and its churning crest. Seth dove into this onrushing wave and allowed it to carry him closer to shore. He was standing up again when two pelicans wheeled overhead and plunged into water. They rested on the surface while swallowing sardines. A gull landed on one pelican's head and tried unsuccessfully to steal part of the catch. The birds left the water and returned to the sky. Seth continued wading until clouds were colored by pink light from the setting sun. The sun turned scarlet before descending into a red haze over the Gulf.

Seth walked to the seafood restaurant near the beach. He put on his sandals and approached this building. The heron was standing on its usual part of the roof. Sethrum went inside and enjoyed a meal of fried grouper accompanied by a tall, sweating glass of draft beer. Upon leaving the restaurant, he threw some snapper fillets onto the roof. The heron outstretched broad wings while stepping toward the food. The bird's long neck snaked forward and the fillets were devoured quickly.

The heron flew to the beach in front of the motel and watched Seth walk to his room. The egret waited on the balcony's railing. In a short time, both birds received a snack of fillets and shrimp. From the sea wall in front of the motel, the heron could peer into Seth's room while the egret snooped from the railing on the balcony. The birds watched Seth pack his equipment.

Mockingbirds were singing in the fresh, gray light of dawn when Seth's truck left the motel's parking lot and started a long journey northward. Although he regretted leaving the Gulf behind, he enjoyed the passing panorama of lakes, rivers, farms and forests. The Smoky Mountains were, as usual, cloaked in a blue haze. The blue tint became darker in the distance. Mountaintops rose above the haze to occasionally become obscured amid drifting clouds. Sethrum traveled as quickly as possible and was pleased to get back to Foxwood.

Upon returning to his cabin, he started a fire in the stove. Next he perked coffee then sat in his favorite chair to rest as he sipped the flavorful drink. The stimulating coffee stirred memories. Reflecting upon his experiences along the Indian trail, he said to himself, I will walk there again in the morning.

THIRTEEN

ATAGA'HI

Robins' songs rang through the dawn. Sethrum walked to the old, hunt cabin. A van was parked at the back of the building and a tendril of smoke drifted away from the chimney.

Although black flies were a nuisance, he pushed onward until he came to the rock where he had received the vision. Without delaying, he soon reached another particularly familiar section. Here, in the vision, he had encountered the Algonkians. The area looked much the same, he thought. The forest is younger now because it has been logged, he said to himself.

Beside the beaver pond, across from the site of the army's encampment, Sethrum built a small fire to get relief from black flies. Looking out over the pond to its opposite shoreline, he thought, I warned the Mohawk village about the impending attack. Tall Pine used a small force to draw the army into a trap. The retreating strategy gave Tall Pine a great victory here.

When Seth arrived at the eastern end of Spirit Lake, he camped on a flat, grassy area where Planter's longhouse had been located. Here he built a cooking fire and put up a small tent. A breeze coming across the lake helped keep away black flies and mosquitoes.

Looking at the flat land around him, Seth recalled the village as it had been. A palisade enclosed the village including the place in the bog where the river came out of the ground. Over two hundred years ago, he reflected, Planter, Corn Tassel and other women would be tending the fields here.

Planter and Tassel would also be making pottery for use in the village as well as for trade. After traveling south, like I did, Planter used one bone impression of a pelican on her pottery while Tassel applied a double print. Planter's pipes had one pelican imprint and Tassel's had two. During a visit to the southern ocean, Planter traded with a Tacobaga woman among the Seminoles. In exchange for arrowheads, Planter received a shell necklace. She gave this necklace to Corn Tassel. Seth's thoughts brought back a clear recollection of Tassel wearing the shell necklace, working at pottery in front of the longhouse. In this place, I became known as Wolf Moon, mused Seth.

Looking around at the area, he thought, this land hasn't changed much. The trees are younger. Water flows from the ground where the Mohawk village once stood. This is the source of the Fox River. The blue, sparking gem of Spirit Lake continues to nestle between wilderness shores consisting of gray rocks topped by white and jack pines.

Scenes from the vision, including spiritual messages he received about his life and this land, all came flooding back to Sethrum. There is a part of my vision I have not yet explored, he reminded himself. My ancestor, the English trader, Ridgeworth Moon, had a cabin and trading post on Sky Mountain. I must see this place. First I have to demolish the Fox Condominium Company.

A quivering wail of a loon came from the lake while the setting sun edged downward, tinting the wilderness with golden sheen. Wolves howled north of the lake. This place reminds me, mused Seth, of the Medicine Lake of the Cherokee. Ataga'hi, the magic lake, is a place where wounded, hunted animals come to heal themselves. All critters need a place like this area in order that they can find rest and heal themselves. People also need such places.

Seth perked coffee and roasted a steak over the fire. Colors of dusk darkened as light diminished with the approach of night. The fire flickered more brightly in the darkness. Wolves howled close to camp. A clear call of a whippoorwill rang through the night as a red edge of the moon appeared above treetops. I must get back and stop the Fox Condominium Company, Seth told himself.

Deciding to not wait until dawn, Seth packed his equipment, poured water on the fire then hurried along the Indian trail, heading southward. The route was outlined by moonlight. He rested beside the beaver pond where the attacking army had camped. A beaver swam across this pond to check light from Sethrum's fire. Sounding the alarm, the beaver slammed its tail down on the water's surface, sending up a white plume of spray. The animal dove beneath ripples glimmering in firelight. The sharp cracking of a branch shot through the solitude before a bear finished climbing down a tree next to camp. The large, dark form dropped to the ground and vanished quickly among shadows.

Having poured water on his fire, Seth continued walking southward along the trail. He walked until one robin sang to be joined by others at daybreak. Accompanied by these songs, he proceeded to his cabin.

After breakfast, he visited Phil and Katherine Dobbs and arranged for the Company to hold an emergency meeting that morning. Only the main partners were called. Seth met these people for the first time when they came to the hastily called talk. Jason Sills was a large, balding man who liked to talk much more than he enjoyed listening. He had become wealthy through shifty, real estate deals. Mabel Templeton was a fat woman who kept much of her shape concealed under loosely fitting clothes. Her hair was combed back from a pasty face with bulbous, green eyes. She had become rich by being willing to move quickly from one business position to another following the highest rate of profit. Casper Forbes was of medium height and build. He always talked loudly and, by being aggressive, had been successful in sales.

The six primary partners of the Fox Condominium Company sat in front of the fireplace containing blazing logs. Sethrum was the farthest back from the fire. While coffee was served and other people talked, Seth looked out a window providing a view of the river. Sunlight danced on the water and illuminated foliage. A light breeze stirred leaves and rippled the water, blending their colors with a golden sheen.

Sethrum was quiet this morning although the other members didn't notice much that was unusual. They were interested in hearing from Sethrum because he had been the founder of the Company and had led attacks against the Wild Society. A feeling of common

Pelican Moon

purpose united the other members. They had come to listen to the person who had started everything.

Phil Dobbs didn't like to delve too deeply into anything. He survived best in the shadow of his wife. He did not look for underlying concerns; but he recognized changes. He was uneasy this morning because he realized that Sethrum had changed. If something bothered Sethrum, then this same problem would soon reach the Company.

Seth was preoccupied with figuring out his strategy. He had to alter everything. I don't like this situation, he told himself. I like to follow a steady course and be trustworthy. On the other hand, when I'm wrong, I must admit I'm wrong. A mistake must not be repeated or continued.

When there was a pause in the conversation, Seth, speaking softly, said, "I would like to tell everyone a story…."

"We've been waiting," interrupted Jason Sills.

"I would like to tell you a story about Ataga'hi," continued Seth.

"Yeah," that's a good one," mocked Jason, sparking laughter.

"Aga who?" asked Casper loudly, continuing the laughter.

"It's a magic lake," said Seth while the others started to note he was actually being serious. "In the Smoky Mountains, there's Ataga'hi, a magic lake," Seth repeated. "The Cherokee know where it is. When an hunter comes near this lake, he knows it by a whirring sound from the wings of thousands of ducks flying about the lake. Upon reaching this place, he would not see it without a vision…."

"You can't be serious, Seth," interrupted Casper. "What're you getting' at?"

"I'm getting to the point," answered Seth. "Because this lake is not always seen, some people think it's not there.

However, it is there if you can see it." Seth stopped talking when he caught a stern, questioning glance from Katherine Dobbs. Phil's mouth was open and he seemed pale. Mabel's eyes looked glazed. The realization came to Seth that these people were not his friends. Suddenly he felt relieved that he would not be letting down people who were his friends. He continued to say, "To one who can see spiritually, such a lake exists and is fed by springs. All kinds of fish and reptiles are in this water. On its surface, or flying overhead, are great flocks of ducks and pigeons. Bears and other animals are on the shore. Ataga'hi is the Medicine Lake of the birds and animals. If hunters wound a bear, the animal makes its way through the woods to this lake and plunges into the water. When the bear comes to the opposite shore, the wounds are healed. For this reason, the lake is kept invisible to many hunters."

"Good story, Seth," said Jason. "Can you tell us what you're getting' at?"

"Yes," answered Seth. "Spirit Lake and Fox River come from water which flows out of the ground at the site of an old, Mohawk village. I have learned a lot from this village. Like the Medicine Lake of Cherokee legend, Spirit Lake, Fox River and the surrounding wilderness are especially spiritual. Visions give us insights into the spiritual side of life regardless of time. I have learned that my idea of developing the Fox River area is a mistake."

"What the…" gasped Casper.

"Other areas," continued Seth, "can be developed. Yet there are places, like this locality, that must be left…."

"Are you joking?" asked Katherine.

"What are you saying anyway?" asked Jason. They were all staring at Seth.

"Enough wilderness has been developed," stated Sethrum. "Wild creatures—and people too—need the remaining wild areas. In such places, there continues a presence of the Creator. Wild places that have survived—some more than others—are like Ataga'hi. They are medicine, or healing, areas. Here animals and people can visit and continue to live. With spiritual insight, we can see such places as being sacred. Thereby, we know them for the first time. I don't worship trees or other parts of the wilderness. But since I know their Creator, I realize that trees, along with other created life forms, are sacred and must not be removed or developed unless such action is absolutely necessary. We don't need the complex I planned for the Fox River. I've been shown a spiritual side of life—of wilderness—and we must treat this remaining, wild land with respect. Some places are more vital than other localities. This Fox River is an essential place. Enough land has been developed. We have to keep our remaining areas of wilderness just as they are."

"I don't know what you're talking about," stated Mabel. Exasperation caused her eyes to bulge more than usual.

"You've been out in the woods too long," said Jason.

"You sound like you've joined the Wild Society," said Phil with his capacity to see things clearly at times.

"I must admit I've come to think—to know—they're right," replied Seth. "I have to say I made a mistake by starting the Fox Condominium Company. This Company should be disbanded now. All partners will be refunded the money they put into this misadventure."

"Hold on now," exclaimed Casper with his face flushed. "The only thing that should be disbanded here is you, Seth. If you want out, we'll buy you out. You can have your money back."

"I own the land where the development was started," retorted Seth.

"With all the lawyers that have been squabbling over this mess," stated Casper, "I know the Company can buy a large tract of river front land north of your old, hunt cabin."

"We can continue the Company by ourselves," said Jason.

"I want in," said Mabel.

"Well, I'm sure in," stated Casper. "The only thing wrong with this Company is Sethrum Moon. Well, he's out. We'll buy him out. The rest of us are staying."

"We're staying with this project," said Katherine. "There's money to be made here and we might as well make it as let someone else move in and do it. You have to take a chance sometimes—especially on a sure thing. Seth has become confused. He's making a mistake. We'll buy him out. That's all there is to it."

"Will Katherine and I still be managing your resort?" Phil softly asked Seth.

"Yes, if you want to," replied Seth.

"We want to," said Phil, looking relieved.

"The only change involved here will be that Foxwood will, from here on, have nothing to do with the Fox Condominium Company," said Seth. "I made a mistake starting this Company; so I'm putting an end to my part in the thing. I'm sorry I made a mistake and misled everyone."

"No one's misled me," said Casper. "The Company's a good idea and we'll keep it going."

"Phil will continue as manager of the Company," added Katherine.

"The only one that's been misled here is Sethrum Moon," said Jason. "The rest of us will carry on the Company. Its land base will just have to move north of the hunt cabin. There's lots o' land there up to and including Spirit Lake." Turning more directly to Seth, Jason said, "I'm sorry you've changed. I prefer the old Sethrum Moon. You were the driving force behind this Company."

"I can drive from here," said Casper. "The new Seth Moon sounds more like a member of the Wild Society and that's a strange turn of events considering he was our attack man against that group."

"As the manager of the Company," said Phil to Seth, "I'll make sure you get your money back. Thanks for keeping us on as managers at Foxwood."

Standing up and starting to leave the room, Seth said, "I'm sorry I made such a mistake; but I wish you all well personally and hope your Company comes to a speedy end."

"You can watch us expand north of your hunt cabin," stated Casper. "From there, we'll develop the whole area including Spirit Lake, your medicine agahooey or whatever you call it. That area is beautiful property. You've joined a lost cause with that Wild Society. We'll get rid o' them too. What can they do anyway?"

"Good luck to you all—personally," said Seth before he left the house.

Walking back to his cabin, Seth thought, I'm finished with the Company. However, I'm also an enemy to the Wild Society. I guess I've made a lot o' mistakes. I'm still the owner of Foxwood and will continue to operate it. Although no one is speaking to me, I, at least, know what I'm doing. I know I'm on the right path. It seems to be a narrow trail to follow. Even Cougar has gone. There're days—and times—like this I guess.

Sethrum walked to his cabin and packed his equipment in preparation for a canoe trip up the Fox River. I must go and see if I can find the trading post built by Ridgeworth on Sky Mountain, Seth said to himself. I know Rid moved from the mountain and started a new trading post here. The new place became Foxwood. I will return to Sky Mountain and see where my tie to this land seems to have started.

FOURTEEN

RIDGEWORTH MOON

Mist from a cold dawn rested above the Fox River when Sethrum got into his canoe and paddled along this stream. Sending ripples across the water, a muskrat swam toward the far bank. An heron flew up from this bank. The elegant bird climbed into a gray sky and flew out of view beyond treetops. A pair of mergansers splashed into flight and flew upstream.

In front of the old cabin, occupied by the Society, there were two loaded canoes. While paddling passed them, Seth thought, I hope they're not going to be traveling upstream.

Rain marked the river's surface. Drops of rain, falling from clouds moving eastward, tapped against Seth's loaded craft. Upon reaching the first rapids, he said to himself, this area will be occupied by the Company. They will be trying to cut down trees in order to start building. The trees are always the first things to be destroyed in the name of progress. I'll have to try to stop such development.

After portaging around the rapids, he paddled to the second portage at the log. A light breeze stirred water and leaves as the canoe moved to the long rapids and the third portage.

While carrying around the long channel, Seth thought, I wonder if the Wild Society members will hear that I've changed. If they hear it, they probably won't believe it. They'll think the whole thing is some kind of a trick. I'll have to watch out for both the Company and the Society.

He paddled to the short rapids. Here a bear looked up from the water's edge. Large jaws held a struggling sucker. This bear, along with two cubs, moved quickly out of sight beyond dense brush.

Having portaged around the short rapids, Seth pushed onward until he came to the stairway rapids where wide sheets of greenish blue water flowed over smooth rocks before tumbling into foaming ridges below each stone step. Seth carried his canoe and equipment for the fifth and last time. He was pleased to finally reach the high, rock camp.

A tall fire, made of dry, pinewood, heated the campsite. Seth spitted a chicken over the flames. A pot of coffee perked at the fire's edge. A tent and sleeping bag were both in place before night's shadows darkened the forest.

When steam shot through breaks in the cooked, golden-colored meat, Seth removed thick, steaming chunks. To them, he added salt and pepper then enjoyed a fine meal followed by coffee.

A whippoorwill's call rang through the woods while Seth rested in his sleeping bag. When the calls stopped, they left a restful solitude. Silence continued until a breeze rustled leaves and swayed boughs. A single cry of a loon came from the north before wolves started howling near camp. Silence returned, allowing welcome sleep to come to Seth.

At dawn, the tent was pounded by rain. It gradually dwindled to drizzle dropping through light fog. Seth packed his equipment into his canoe then kept warm by paddling. While the craft proceeded along the river, the land became flat and included a section of sandy banks topped by verdant grasses. Paddling steadily, he reached the widening in the river. Cries of sea gulls greeted him at the lake. He crossed to its north shore and carried his canoe up onto the top of a rocky hill. This height of land provided a view of most of the lake. A steady breeze helped to remove black flies. He camped here for the night then heated beans for breakfast next morning.

Having prepared one pack of essential supplies along with his tent, sleeping bag, axe, knife and rifle, Seth was ready to travel. There isn't much of a trail around here, he thought. But I'm sure I know where I'm going. Tall Pine, Planter and Corn Tassel said a trail left this site and went directly north to a low mountain where Ridgeworth Moon had built a cabin at the base of a cliff. I can use my compass to make sure I am heading directly to the north.

Sethrum traveled steadily throughout the day. At dusk, he selected a camping place on an high, rocky area where a breeze would help remove black flies. He first set up his tent and sleeping bag then prepared bannock, completing this meal with coffee. A whippoorwill spoke repeatedly from a forest of shadows while Seth sipped coffee contentedly.

He slept during the first part of the night. Since there were no flies around, he decided to travel by moonlight. He packed his equipment and left the comfortable camp. Walking at a steady pace, he followed open areas of rock and game trails as much as possible. The needle of his compass helped to keep him heading north in the pale light.

Dawn found Sethrum on high ground overlooking a series of beaver ponds. After sleeping until the sun was well up into the sky, he started the day with a meal of bannock followed by coffee.

By late afternoon, Seth had reached the mountain. Forested hills climbed upward into a dome-shaped height of land called Sky Mountain. Near its summit, as Tall Pine had mentioned, there was a cliff. Ridgeworth Moon had built his cabin, trading post at the base of the rock face, recalled Seth.

He camped where he could see the cliff. A tall fire helped to drive away the flies. He made pancakes and coffee while the setting sun flashed red light on the mountain and its cliff. An eagle screamed from red clouds overhead. Wolves seemed to answer. After night's shadows had gathered upon the land, the clear calls of a whippoorwill rang through the forest.

Following a breakfast of bannock and coffee, Sethrum stepped out into morning sunlight and started the last part of his journey to Sky Mountain. Occasionally, during this upward walk, he came upon sections of an old trail that had been described by Tall Pine. The most distinct sections of this path led directly toward the cliff.

At the base of the rock face, Sethrum found no remnants of a cabin. However, on a sandy promontory, a short distance out from the cliff, overlooking a panorama of wilderness to the south, he found a partial outline of an old, stone foundation. A stone base was covered by rotted wood concealing hand-hewn beams.

Seth removed enough rotten wood to ease himself down passed a beam to a sandy floor. In the northeastern corner of the foundation, there was a cistern. All parts of this basement had been constructed with closely fitting rocks. An opening in a central wall led to a carefully built cellar where food had likely been stored.

The eastern chamber, like the rest of the structure, had a sandy floor. Beams, overlapped by decayed wood, formed a rough ceiling. Natural, rock ledges provided shelves containing rotted boxes.

Seth moved slowly, checking the murkiness for animals that might be living in the ruins. This would be a great place for rattlers or bears, he warned himself. I'll be in real trouble if there's a wolverine in here. At such a time as this I'd like to have a dog to check out the place.

A shiver ran across Seth's skin as he got a feeling of stepping back through time over two hundred years. Maybe such places should be left alone, he told himself. Ridgeworth Moon would have taken most of his trade goods and other supplies to his new trading post that became Foxwood. He changed locations because the Mohawk village moved farther south. Likely, he didn't fully abandon this place. It probably continued to be his home—one of his two homes.

On the shelves, some decayed wood seemed to be remnants of old boxes. More rotten wood along with sand, dust and animal as well as bird droppings covered the boxes. Porcupines and owls have been in here, noted Seth. Having removed some debris, he poked cautiously in the first box and uncovered a stash of clay, trade pipes. A second, larger bin contained copper kettles. Remnants of metal were in another section of containers. A top, separate ledge held pottery bowls along with pipes.

Sethrum reached up and removed a pipe from a layering of sandy dust. Dust dropped to the floor, leaving fine particles shimmering in the air. He blew away a remaining film. A tremor ran through him when he saw a double pelican imprint located where the pipe stem met the bowl. His hands trembled as he checked the other pipes. They were marked with either one or two pelican designs.

He was feeling eerily nervous and his heart pounded when he reached for the first bowl. Again, he blew away a coating of dust. Along with lined patterns on the lip and neck, there was a row of dots bordering the shoulder. A circular, bone impression showing an outline of a pelican had also been added to the neck. Reaching for a second bowl, then blowing off the sandy dust, he found himself staring at a bone imprint of two pelicans. Rid Moon, said Seth to himself, traded for the pottery bowls and pipes of Planter and Corn Tassel.

Seth replaced the pottery bowls and pipes except for one pipe containing the double pelican design. He also picked up a trade pipe from a decayed box. After putting these two pipes into his pocket, he checked the remainder of the main room where decaying beams and other wood covered the ceiling. A small stream of water trickled into the cistern. From his pack, he removed his coffeepot and dipped it into the stone walled basin and obtained clear water. He went outside and placed this pot at the edge of an old fireplace in front of the foundation. Dry kindling was next piled inside a circle of blackened stones. Flames flickered upward and were soon dancing light across a side of the foundation.

While waiting for the coffee to perk, Seth reached into his pocket and withdrew the two pipes. He crumbled a cigar in his hands and used this tobacco to fill the pipes.

Having filled the pelican pipe, he admired its lines and artistic construction. I wonder if I saw her making this pipe, Seth mused while bringing a burning stick to the tobacco. The tobacco ignited quickly, sending a tendril of bluish-gray smoke curling skyward. He smoked this pipe contentedly and watched a majestic panorama of wilderness. His thoughts went back to the village, particularly the place in front of the longhouse where Tassel worked.

Behind the foundation, the rock face reached upward to a crest of white pines. On the other three sides of the cabin site, slopes undulated down to generally flat terrain. All of this area was densely forested. Spruce formed a spiked carpet mottled by rounded clumps of deciduous trees or pines. Clouds drifted over the mountain while dropping stands of mist down to a receding carpet of trees. This country hasn't changed much through the years, reflected Seth before he sent a tendril of smoke winding toward clouds. *I found part of the old trail that Tall Pine described, connecting this place with the Mohawk village. He said there were other trails leading out from the base of the cliff, heading east and west. I will rebuild this cabin just as it was over two hundred years ago. I can use much of the original foundation as well as the cistern. With money I'm removing from the Company, I'll buy land here to protect this site. I would like to live here.*

Seth pitched his tent between the foundation and the campfire. After preparing his sleeping bag and checking other supplies, he sat down to sip some coffee. *I can repair the stone foundation,* he reasoned. *Many ceiling beams are in useable condition. I'll have to replace the rest of the building. With the foundation and its ceiling restored, I'll return to Foxwood and use my funds from the Company to buy this land. I'll have to hire an helicopter to bring in equipment like a wood stove and windows.

Having formulated a plan, he got his axe and went to work. His efforts were steady and methodical. The tapping or chopping of an axe became common sounds on the mountain and gradually lost any worrying impact on birds or animals. He selected logs carefully in order to not mar the surrounding view of a sprawling, rugged expanse of wilderness. A trail of smoke continually curled upward from a campfire in front of the foundation.

After clearing away all debris, he first checked foundation stones, securing those that had become loose and replacing others that had fallen. He removed decayed wood and used it, like other debris, to feed the fire. New beams were cut. They would be put in place when he obtained some hauling equipment.

When most of the basement materials had been prepared, Sethrum sat down beside his fire. He rested while drinking coffee. I'll have to get an helicopter to bring in boards for the floor, he thought. I'll also need boards and more beams for the rest of the building. I'll use an helicopter to bring in all necessary supplies including some logs.

A pair of eagles frequently soared above the mountain. Hawks circled over the lower forest. Deer were numerous as were most other animals and birds.

When Sethrum left his new, mountain home, he knew he would be back soon. He walked south, trying to follow the old trail as closely as possible. In some soft areas of humus and moss, the path was deeply indented and could be detected easily. Such links joined invisible sections that crossed rocks or watery expanses. Although the terrain varied, the route's direction ran continuously to the south. Seth was always pleased to recognize landmarks and particularly welcomed the high rocks bordering the north shore of Spirit Lake. His feeling of contentment vanished after he climbed to the top of the rocky hill. Below, on the shore, he saw his canoe. It had been placed beside two of the Society's canoes next to two tents.

Looking down at the campsite, Seth thought, I'm stuck without my canoe. They know that. They will also have my other equipment. I'll rest for a while before I visit them tonight and recover my gear. They have left me with no choice.

Seth selected a dry, comfortable place among exposed roots of a white pine. He stretched out here and soon was asleep. He woke up a few times and observed the lower camp. A large fire flickered light across tents, canoes and four men. The men had caught and filleted fish then had a fish fry followed by a time of beer drinking and talking around the fire. Afterward, the camp became quiet. A man occasionally emerged from a tent and sat beside the warming fire before returning to the shelter to sleep.

When Seth woke up at dawn, he started to worry that he had slept too long. Gray light seeping through the forest enabled him to clearly distinguish outlines of objects.

He quickly gathered his traveling equipment and hastened toward the lower camp. He approached it cautiously and quietly. Embers glowed in the fireplace. Dawn's light filtered through a still, cool forest disturbed only by snoring sounds coming occasionally from one tent.

Seth picked up his canoe and slipped it into the water. Next he put the paddles inside. Seeing the rest of his equipment stashed with firewood under a tarpaulin, he quickly recovered these packs and placed them in his canoe. Having finished the work, he relaxed enough to add water to a pot of strong coffee. The pot had been kept beside the fire and was warmed by its embers.

He enjoyed heat from the embers while he sipped bitter coffee. Breaking the silence with a loud squawk, an heron flew over the lake. This one squawk was followed by a long, plaintive cry of a loon. Snoring sounds came again from the tent.

Seth finished a cupful of the coffee. The dawn is the best time o' the day, he reflected as he walked to the water's edge. He stepped into his craft, sat down and started paddling through mist hanging above the calm lake.

He paddled east to the outlet of Fox River where the river's current tugged at the canoe, helping to bring it downstream to the stairway rapids. He steered into a center flow and was carried above smooth rocks before being dropped into a thrashing turbulence leading to more rocks. After getting bumped and dropped along the stairway descent, the canoe followed a winding path of water leading to the short rapids. Seth shot through the rapids and paddled along a calmer section of river winding passed flat, rocky banks. The craft entered the narrow channel and was drawn quickly down the long rapids before reaching another calm stretch of water. Seth had to portage around the log. He successfully steered through the last rapids where the Company planned to start a development complex. Although there were no canoes stashed near the hunt cabin, a film of smoke wound away from the stone chimney.

Upon arriving at his cabin, Sethrum wasted no time in carrying out his plans. Meeting almost immediately with Phil Dobbs, Seth completed the withdrawal of his money from the Company. Bolstered by this capital, he went to a real estate broker and was able to purchase the land he required at Sky Mountain. He also arranged to have an helicopter deliver building supplies to the cabin site. When he was driving back to his cabin, everything seemed to be in order until he was forced to drive onto the shoulder of the road to allow for the passage of a swiftly moving line of police cars.

FIFTEEN

THE BLOCKADE

Keeping the police cars in view most of the time, Sethrum followed them to a chain roadblock which the Society had put across a lane leading to property beside the first rapids on the Fox River where the Company was going to start its development. The Company had hired a crew to clear land near the rapids. In response, the Society chained off the lane and stopped tree cutters from entering the site. While lawyers carried the dispute through the legal system, the two groups clashed in front of the blockade.

On each side of the roadblock, fires provided people with places to get warm and also do some cooking. Most of the fighting was stopped by the arrival of the police. A stand off resulted at the chain as well as in court.

Sethrum Moon kept his distance from both groups. Additional people kept arriving, offering support to both sides and expanding the problem. Seth talked mainly with the police. He visited their campfires to get coffee.

Selecting a tall, white pine near the blockade, Seth was able to sit down at the base of this tree and watch each encampment. South of the chain, there were vans belonging to the cutting crew. Workers gathered in this area. Company members along with their supporters came to the same site. They had cooking fires where food as well as coffee could be obtained along with information. A mobile, food truck supplied extra snacks and drinks. North of the line, the Society had cooking fires. A growing number of Society members and supporters assembled near these fires. As the

Pelican Moon

crowds increased so did the struggle. The police resorted to using horses and dogs to keep the groups apart.

Two trucks, coming from the south, pushed against the chain and broke it. They proceeded to move slowly through a wall of Society supporters. Drivers and other people were pulled out of the trucks before the vehicles were torched. They were engulfed in whooshing balls of flames, sending columns of black smoke into the clear sky. A general fight erupted. Using horses and dogs, the police gradually separated the two mobs. Fire fighters extinguished the blazes. The charred vehicles were towed away. Following this larger flash point, as with smaller skirmishes, the two sides withdrew and regrouped around their own campfires.

Sethrum usually remained near the base of the white pine. By sitting on exposed roots and leaning his back against the trunk, he rested while sipping coffee and watching the blockade. The Company people hoped he would continue to not take an active part. The police were pleased he visited their campfires rather than joining one of the other groups. The Society people distrusted rumors he had changed and broken away from the Company he had started. They also noticed he kept much to himself and smoked clay or pottery pipes commonly used at the time of the fur trade.

Seth used a twig to remove ashes from the bowl of the clay pipe. Everything seemed to have settled down to a routine around the fires. People talked in their own, separate gatherings. He reached inside his jacket's pocket and withdrew a double pelican pipe along with a small pouch of tobacco and a lighter. Working slowly and skillfully, he filled the bowl with tobacco. A wooden match was used to ignite the tobacco, causing a whiff of fragrant smoke to curl upward. He leaned back

Pelican Moon

against the pine trunk to smoke this pipe and enjoy the memories it stirred.

During his observations of the people at the barricade, Seth noted that one of the Society members seemed to be particularly interested in the old pipes. This person watched with binoculars when one of the pipes was being smoked. The pelican pipe stirred the most attention. Following one, longer period of focusing binoculars on this pipe, the man walked over to talk to Taisse Cantry. As they talked, they both looked in Seth's direction.

Taisse turned abruptly away from the man, as if she had been angered by what he had said. Seeming determined to settle something, she walked directly toward Seth.

Approaching Seth, her eyes flashed with hostility when she asked, "How'd you get my pipe?"

"This can't be yours," he replied calmly, surprised by her anger.

"Can I check it?" she asked reaching toward it.

"Sure," he answered, giving her the pipe. She held it carefully as if accustomed to such things. She appeared to be fascinated by it.

"A pottery pipe with two pelicans," she said evenly. Her eyes were clear, brown and accusing. "This is mine," she stated. "I'm the only one who has these pipes."

"I guess you're the only one other than myself," said Seth, amazed that she seemed to know about the pelicans. "If you check your pipes, you will find that none of them are missing."

"How did you get it?" she demanded, taking another look at the pelican design.

"I found it," he said.

"Where did you find it?" she asked.

"On my land at a trading post built by my ancestor, Ridgeworth Moon," he said.

Pelican Moon

"You're related to him?" she asked as her anger clearly changed to curiosity.

"Yes," he replied.

"You found the trading post?" she asked again.

"Yes," he said. "As you probably know, it's on Sky Mountain."

"You own some land on Sky Mountain?" she asked.

"I bought it because Ridgeworth had his trading post there," he said. "I'm rebuilding the cabin and I'm going to live there."

Seth was surprised when Taisse calmly returned the pipe. He tried smoking it and a wisp of smoke ascended from the bowl. "How did you get these pipes?" he asked her.

Taisse turned away deliberately and gracefully, as she seemed to do most things. She walked back to the Society line.

The man with the binoculars met her. "Is everything all right?" he asked.

"Yes," she answered without stopping. She approached Sal Perkins who was refilling her cup with coffee.

"Can I get some for you?" asked Sal.

"No, thanks," said Taisse. "Will you come with me? I want to talk to Sethrum Moon."

"Sethrum Moon?" she asked, looking astonished. Her mouth partly opened. Her eyes questioned.

"Yes," replied Taisse.

She always seems composed, thought Sal, even when she's doing something foolish. "Just the two of us?" asked Sal.

"Yes," answered Taisse. She waited patiently, fully expecting Sal to come with her. More words were unnecessary and would just delay things.

"You know what you're doing?" asked Sal.

"Yeah," she answered with a smile.

"Now?" asked Sal, delaying.

Taisse nodded her head and waited. Not being able to put things off any longer, Sal carried her cup of coffee and walked with Taisse. They reached the base of the pine just as Seth finished emptying ashes from the bowl of the pipe. Seth noticed that an handle of a gun protruded from an holster inside Sal's jacket. "You don't take any chances, do you?" he said to Sal.

"No," she answered. "Taisse is taking this chance."

"Will you come with us?" Taisse asked Seth. "There's something I'd like to show you."

"Okay," he replied. He stood up and started following the two women. Other vehicles have blocked in my truck, said Seth to himself as he left the congested roadway behind. I'll get my truck later. Taisse seems to be heading toward my hunt cabin. I wonder how she found out about the pipes.

The women stayed ahead of Sethrum. Sal asked Taisse, "What's this all about?"

"I'll show you," answered Taisse.

"Did you give him a pipe?" asked Sal.

"No," said Taisse. "I think that's his."

"How would he get it?" questioned Sal.

"That's what we're goin' to talk about," said Taisse as she led the way to the hunt cabin. The sun was setting in a spray of golden light. Black flies were a nuisance.

Upon approaching the cabin's back door, Seth noted the usual van parked behind the building. Other vans and cars were also present. A light brightened the kitchen window. Taisse opened the door and walked inside followed by Sal then Seth.

A large man, working at a counter, turned pale when he saw Seth. Picking up a frying pan, the man muttered, "What the…."

"You won't be needin' that, Perdy," said Taisse. "He's with us."

"Oh, he's with you and that makes it all right," stated Perdy sarcastically as his face flushed. "Well maybe it's not all right with me."

Holding the pan grimly and starting to come around the counter, he stopped abruptly when Sal stated, "Not now." Frustration brought a film of sweat to Perdy's face. "Maybe later," added Sal with a grin, trying to defuse the guy.

Turning to Seth, Taisse said, "Sethrum Moon, meet Perdy Willis."

"I've met the…." muttered Perdy.

"I've had the pleasure too," said Seth tensely.

"If that…." continued Perdy.

Cutting him off again, Sal said, "Leave it. We'll call you if we need you."

"Maybe I'll just help anyway," he persisted.

"No, you won't," stated Sal.

With a scowl on his face, Perdy put the frying pan on the counter and went back to the work he had been doing. Seth followed the two women to the front room where logs blazed in a fireplace occupying much of the east wall. He sat down on a couch next to the south wall. Sal sat down on a couch along the west side of the room. Taisse walked to a room adjoining the hallway. She returned carrying a large box and she placed it on the floor in front of Sal. "That thing's heavy," she exclaimed to Sal. "Don't open it yet," Taisse added. She left again and came back with glasses of beer. She served beer before sitting down next to Sal.

Turning to Seth, Taisse said, "Can I have the pipe?"

Seth stood up, walked toward Taisse. From his pocket, he removed the beautifully designed pipe and gave it to her. "Are you a collector of some kind?" he asked.

"No," she replied, holding the pipe carefully. "I'm only interested in this pipe. How did you get it?"

While Taisse continued examining the pipe, Seth sat down again, drank some beer then said, "Around the year 1720, there was a Mohawk village at the eastern end of Spirit Lake where the Fox River flows out of the ground. At that village, there was a chief, called Tall Pine. He, his wife, Planter, and their daughter, Corn Tassel, along with others, had traveled south to the ocean and met some Seminoles. Among the Seminoles, there was a Tocobaga woman. To this woman, Planter gave flint arrowheads in exchange for a shell necklace." Noticing the fascinated look on Taisse's face, Seth hesitated before saying, "Planter gave the shell necklace to her daughter, Corn Tassel. Both women liked pelicans. The women were also great potters. Planter designed and used an impression of one pelican on all her pottery bowls and pipes. Tassel used a double pelican design.

North of the Mohawk village, an English trader, called Ridgeworth Moon, built a cabin that was also a trading post. It was located on Sky Mountain. From there, he traded with the Mohawk village. In the course of his work, he traded for bowls and pipes made by Planter and Tassel. He kept some of this prized pottery, along with other trade items, in the cellar of his cabin. When the Mohawk village moved south, Ridgeworth built a cabin and trading post at the location of Foxwood. He likely continued to use each cabin. The southern place later became the resort it is today.

Through the years, my family lost ownership of Foxwood. I worked there as an handy man until I won enough money at the dog races to buy the place from Katherine and Phil. They continue to be managers. With remaining money, I started the Fox Condominium Company to develop the Fox River. After learning more about this particular wilderness, I realized I had made a mistake in wanting to develop the area. I tried to disband the Company; but the other partners wanted to keep the thing operating. Therefore, I left the Company and used

Pelican Moon

the money to buy land and start rebuilding the cabin on Sky Mountain. In the cellar of Rid's cabin, I found bowls and pipes. They had been made by both Planter and Tassel because each piece contained an imprint of either a single or double pelican. That's how I got Tassel's pipe."

Taisse stood up. She walked to the kitchen and returned with a can of beer for each person. After they had refilled their glasses, Taisse said, "My grandmother was Mohawk. She did pottery work and had received pelican designed, pottery bowls, along with pipes, that had been handed down to her mother. My grandmother handed down to me the original, pelican-marked bowls and pipes. She also taught me to do pottery work. On my pottery, I put the double, pelican designs."

Seth stared at Taisse and, for the first time, realized how much she reminded him of Tassel. "Tassel is your ancestor?" he asked while he thought he saw only similarities between Taisse and Tassel.

"Yes," she answered. "And Ridgeworth Moon is your ancestor?" she asked.

"Yes," he said.

"We should have met earlier," she exclaimed after she put down her glass. She went to the box, opened it and took out a pottery bowl marked with a single, pelican impression. "These are originals from my grandmother," explained Taisse, handing the bowl to Seth.

"It's just like the others made by Planter," he said.

"How do you know that?" asked Taisse.

"There are some of these in the cellar of Rid's cabin," he said.

"Oh, yes, I forgot you said that," she said as if she was in a trance.

"You know," said Seth, shocked by a sort of spell gripping him, in Florida, I met a woman who said she had a friend in the north who puts pelican designs on her pottery."

"Sihoki?" asked Taisse incredulously.

"Yes," answered Seth, staring at her.

"I've been to see her," she exclaimed. "We work on pottery." Returning to the box, Taisse brought out a bowl marked with the double pelican design. Seth gave the first bowl to Sal and received the second bowl from Taisse. She saw Seth's hands shake when he noted the double pelican marks. From the box, Taisse also removed pottery pipes decorated with either a single or double pelican pattern. Taisse held the pipe Seth had been smoking and placed it in her hand next to a double, pelican pipe from the box. The pipes seemed to be identical. "They look like they have been made by the same person," said Taisse more to herself than to Seth.

Afterward, Taisse brought out some of her own pottery pieces and they matched the originals. She said, "My grandmother gave me the original bowls and pipes. She taught me to make pottery. I have a studio where I do pottery work at my house in town."

"Did your grandmother, by any chance, hand down to you a shell necklace?" asked Seth.

"How would...?" whispered Taisse. She left the room. When she returned, Seth stared at her in disbelief, as if he was going back over two hundred years, seeing both Tassel and Taisse. She was wearing the shell necklace. "My grandmother," she said, "told me the owner of this necklace had given it to one of her daughters. It was passed down to my grandmother then to me."

Taisse untied the necklace and handed it to Seth. He held it carefully. His hands shook again when he saw, carved in shell, the name Wolf Moon. "I didn't know she did that," said Seth.

"What did you say?" asked Taisse who had become fascinated by all of Seth's reactions.

"There's a name carved in the necklace," answered Seth.

"Yes," said Taisse. "It's Wolf Moon. Maybe Wolf is what they called Rid."

"Yeah, maybe," replied Seth.

"You act like your name is Wolf," said Taisse. She was smiling slightly; but she was serious too.

"It is," he replied.

"Are you the one who got his name carved on this necklace?" she asked, smiling.

"Yes," he answered seriously.

"Yeah, sure," she said, smiling again and staring at him. "You really get around, don't you. So you're called Wolf Moon?"

"A long time ago," he replied. "And you were called Corn Tassel."

Not wanting to think about his comment right away, she said, "My other ancestors are English. Among some of their records, that I have at home, there is mention of Ridgeworth Moon. Apparently he became quite popular when a relative who worked with him warned the Mohawk village of an impending attack. This person's name was Wolf Moon. I carry on the traditions for my grandmother. I also do other pottery work."

"I have records too," said Seth. "I'll tell you about them some day." Returning the shell piece to her, he added, "Here's your necklace. "I'm going back to my cabin. Thanks for showing me these things. You can keep the pipe. I have others at the Sky Mountain site. I can also share with you more pottery pipes—and bowls. I would just like to keep some of each for the memories."

Having returned the pottery pieces and necklace, Seth walked to the front door. He opened it and said, "Thanks for the beer. I'll be talking to you again about these things."

He stepped outside and was just closing the door behind him when Taisse called out, "Wolf Moon." He froze then walked away, heading toward his cabin.

SIXTEEN

COUGAR'S RACE

Sethrum Moon went to work at his cabin site on Sky Mountain. Building supplies were delivered by helicopter. Sounds of chopping, hammering and sawing echoed across the land. Ravens frolicked overhead and seemed to be attracted to the construction work in addition to the food put out for them on a prominent rock. A bear arrived to check the noise as did a few foxes and wolves. Animals and birds became accustomed to activity near the base of the cliff. Some members of the Wild Society helped Seth with the work. He gave them the old, hunt cabin for their headquarters.

One afternoon, while other workers were resting out of hearing distance from Seth and Taisse, she asked him how he found out about Tall Pine, Planter and Corn Tassel. Although Seth seldom talked about his vision, he told Taisse about it.

Sethrum shared his supply of pottery with Taisse. "Some day," she said, "I will show you how to make pottery. Maybe we could expand the business. On all our pottery pieces, we would place the design of the circular bone impression containing the pelican, resembling a pelican gliding in front of the moon. This imprint has a long history and is continuing. I like the design and call it the pelican moon.

Although the cabin work took place successfully, nothing ran smoothly for Society members at the blockade. They couldn't compete with the Company's money and influence. The Society's obstruction of development was declared to be illegal. Society lawyers tried to get this decision changed and the barricade stayed in place.

Like many Society members, Sethrum was kept busy with work at the cabin site and the Society's headquarters in the hunt cabin. The blockade was also continued. His routine was interrupted by a telephone call from the South. Sihoki called to tell Seth when Cougar would be running in his first race.

Following the message from Sihoki, Seth put a few supplies in his truck then drove south. His journey took him along highways bordered by lush foliage and bountiful crops along with forests and mountains. Clouds concealed peaks of the Smoky Mountains when Seth passed through this area on his way to warmer regions in the south.

Upon reaching the Blue Heron Motel, he went to the ocean for a swim. He checked the usual assortment of shells while scaled sardine minnows darted away at his approach. Larger fish swam passed in deeper, bluish green water.

Pelicans glided overhead, occasionally diving to get fish. Stingrays slithered away from Seth when he waded back to shore. He used his net to catch minnows to feed the egret and heron. Both of these birds remembered Seth and followed him along the beach.

Having fed the birds and rested among the timeless rhythms of waves breaking along the shore, Seth drove to the racetrack. He placed only one bet—Cougar to win. Next he bought beer and went to see the dogs being led by leadouts toward the starting gate.

One dog stopped, turned and moved so swiftly toward Seth that he saw only a grayish blur until he was hit by Cougar and knocked over backwards. Beer sprayed in an arc above the dog stopping on top of Seth. Pushing through an astonished crowd, the leadout recovered Cougar and they both ran to follow the others to the starting gate.

Seth bought more beer before returning to the same place. The band played and dogs barked shrilly. The band finished playing. The dogs became silent. A mechanical rabbit moved along the track, approaching the starting gate.

Seth gulped his beer as a blur of dogs swarmed out of the gate. They moved like one creature with many legs. At the clubhouse turn, the creature stumbled, spitting two dogs away from the pack. One dog returned to follow the group. The second dog came out of a summersault facing backwards and kept running. This dog turned sharply, almost falling again then jumped the rail and ran at Seth, hitting him with a yelp and a rambunctious greeting. Getting knocked over again, Seth stood up, ran with Cougar to the entrance and they both left the building. Getting into the truck, Seth, with Cougar on the passenger seat, drove off the parking lot and traveled back to the motel.

At the motel, Seth packed his possessions, put fish out for the heron and egret then returned to his truck. The dog took his usual place on the front, passenger seat. He watched the other vehicles and roadsides while Seth drove to the riverside home of Sihoki Panther.

"I've heard all about it," exclaimed Sihoki after she had given Cougar water and poured beer for Seth along with herself. "The track called and everything has been straightened out. Track officials phoned me. They told me Cougar had bolted from the race and left with a man in a truck. I told them not to worry because the man was the dog's owner and Cougar had just retired from racing."

Sihoki's eyes sparkled as Seth told her again about Cougar's first race. "The guys at the track were laughing when they called," she said. "Obviously Cougar was not being stolen because the dog ran with you. You were wise to get Cougar out of there and we would straighten things out later. His race

Pelican Moon

was of course over. For Cougar, there's at least one thing—one person—more important than racing. The dog's happy and that's all we want."

Seth and Cougar left Sihoki's home and traveled northward. They visited Will Panther in the mountains and Seth told him about Cougar's short racing career. Continuing his journey northward, Seth's thoughts kept returning to Cougar's race. Yes, he was fast, Seth noted with satisfaction. Cougar fell and could have recovered had he been going in the right direction and not left the race. He could be a champion, according to Sihoki. But Sihoki and I both agreed that the dog's heart wasn't in racing. He had found a home with Sethrum Moon.

SEVENTEEN

THE SPRING

Sethrum and Cougar returned to the cabin at Foxwood. When they entered the room, Cougar circled the room and barked at Seth as if the period of absence had all been Seth's fault. After complaining loudly, the suddenly contented dog went over to the bear rug, stretched out and went to sleep.

He's happy now, thought Seth before he sat in his favorite chair to enjoy a cup of green tea. I'm also pleased to have Cougar's company again. We have to go to Sky Mountain.

The next morning, sunlight brightened a rain-soaked forest. Songs of robins and cardinals rang through the mist.

Seth slipped his canoe onto the Fox River. Cougar took his place in the bow. Having loaded the equipment, Seth stepped into his craft and sat down in his comfortable place at the stern. He dipped and turned his paddle while pushing it through calm water, sending the canoe forward. Ripples spread outward toward each bank when the canoe moved upstream. An heron watched from shore near two canoes pulled up in front of the Society's headquarters.

Sethrum proceeded along the familiar river. He made the usual five portages, camped on the high rock above the stairway rapids and reached Spirit Lake during the second day.

Sea gulls rested on rocks along the water's edge. Emitting a tumult of calls, other gulls wheeled overhead, etched in sunlight against a backdrop of a pale, blue sky. Sethrum paddled to the east shore. Always accompanied by Cougar, Seth walked around the site of the old, Mohawk village. The area brought back memories in such a rush he almost thought he was again back in time, visiting the active village. He came to the place, inside the village, where the Fox River emerged from the ground. Watching water flowing from the earth, he said to himself, the Fox River comes from the Mohawk village. Lastly, he visited the place where Planter and Corn Tassel worked on pottery in front of their longhouse.

Seth returned to his canoe and paddled to the north shore. Back from the water, he hid his canoe along with supplies that could not be carried at one time. Cougar eagerly led the way along the north trail. A two-day journey brought them to the cliff on Sky Mountain.

A setting sun shot golden light onto the rock face and new cabin. Walking toward this cabin, Seth enjoyed the grandeur of the amber light coloring clouds drifting above forested, downward-undulating slopes leading to distant lowlands. A bear ambled out of view east of the cabin. A quivering cry of an eagle came from the top of the cliff.

Upon entering the building's back door, Seth and Cougar were greeted by a resinous fragrance of pine pitch. A stone fireplace occupied much of the north wall. Along the western side, there were two bedrooms next to a kitchen. Two more bedrooms in addition to a bathroom took up most of the east wall. The building had two windows on each wall along with a front and back door and a wood stove in the center of the main room facing south over the mountainside. A cabin in the clouds, reflected Seth as he admired the structure. He placed a bear rug for Cougar at the base of the east wall between the bedrooms.

Sethrum placed birch bark in the wood stove. On top of this bark, he dropped kindling topped by dry, birch wood. He lit the bark and a diminutive flame grew larger while climbing through kindling then along the wood. Flames soon blazed in the stove sending heat throughout the cabin. Seth sat on a chair located on the western side of the stove. After lighting his pipe, he sensed a warm, contended feeling of knowing he was home.

In the southwest and southeast corners, trapdoors led to a cellar constructed of stone. Followed by a vanishing tendril of smoke from his pipe, Seth went down to the cellar. He lit an oil lamp. Its yellow light brightened rock ledges on stone walls topped by a strongly beamed ceiling. The natural ledges contained boxes of trade goods together with tools and other equipment. A cistern, located in the northeast corner, continued to supply cool, clear water. Food was stored on the western half of the cellar.

Pelican Moon

Reaching up to one of the natural ledges, Sethrum carefully removed a pottery bowl marked by one, circular, pelican imprint. As Taisse said, he thought, the design looks like a pelican gliding in front of the moon. She continues to use the same imprint and calls it the pelican moon. It's included in the rim pattern consisting of lines and dots incised in the clay.

He carried the bowl upstairs and put it on the mantel above the fireplace. Beside this first bowl, he placed one with a double pelican impression. Next he added pottery pipes containing both single and double pelicans. Lastly, he put clay, trade pipes on the mantel. Now the place is finished, he said to himself. I have a few spare pieces of pottery in the cellar and have given the others to Taisse. Next to the old pottery, he placed similar works made by Taisse. Also, around the room, he positioned contemporary pieces of Taisse's pottery.

Sethrum and Cougar wandered along old trails on the mountainside as well as on the lower terrain. For the next few days, the man and dog explored the surrounding area, seeing birds and animals such as bears, hawks and eagles. Smoke ascending from a stone chimney on the cabin at Sky Mountain marked a trail in the sky indicating that the cabin had come back to life after having been unoccupied for over two hundred years.

Leaving their mountain home, Sethrum followed Cougar along the path to Spirit Lake. The canoe was again loaded for a return trip down the river. Paddling was easy because the current helped to bring the craft to the cabin at Foxwood.

Seth arrived in time to see the end of the blockade. All legal proceedings had gone against the Wild Society. Tree cutters were to be allowed to start clearing land.

Beside the first rapids, a tall, white pine had been marked with red tape. This tree was to be cut down to signify the start of the development project.

On the appointed day for the first cutting of a tree, a crowd gathered. Sethrum, Taisse and other Society members were present along with the Company people and curious supporters for both sides. The news media were ready to record the end of a long and bitter dispute.

The event became a time of celebration for the Company. A pancake breakfast was served. Speeches were made. A small band imposed its music on the forest. Society members acquiesced to this event. The struggle had been long. They were not sure of how to proceed although their opposition would continue.

One of the tree cutters started a chain saw, filling the immediate area with erratic noise and blue smoke. He used this saw to make an horizontal cut on the tree's side facing the rapids of the Fox River. Between blasts from the saw, a finch and cardinal could be heard singing from the tops of neighboring trees. A fish splashed in a pool below the rapids, directly in front of the tree.

The saw made a second cut, starting above and angled down to meet the first cutting. When a chunk of wood was removed from the cut area, a wedge-shaped space was left in the trunk. The tree's branches were etched against an azure sky. Ravens called. A robin sang from the woods.

The tree cutters moved around to the opposite side of the trunk. They started a third cut, angling it down toward the point of the wedge-shaped opening. The saw roared, spewing out blue smoke and sawdust.

The saw was removed so the men could check the progress of their work. The Society people had always been doubtful about tolerating this tree cutting ceremony. They knew their protest would continue. This ceremony was only one loss and there had been many such setbacks.

A wedge was placed into the cut at the back of the tree. This wedge was pounded into the opening. Next the saw was inserted between the wedge and the uncut part of the trunk. The saw was roaring again, spewing out more chips and smoke, when a sharp cracking sound came from the trunk's base. The tree shook. A few people in the crowd cheered. The tree moved. Its top branches swayed forward. They faltered, hesitated then proceeded onward slowly. Picking up speed, they arced downward in a whooshing, cracking fall that plunged the full length of the tree into the Fox River. The white pine hit with an explosion of spray and broken branches.

Churned water gradually settled over the trunk as well as most of its branches. Some people cheered. Reporters moved closer for pictures.

While people watched the river, water kept swirling over the tree. In a short time, the water changed and moved under the trunk. Soon the surface of the river was lower than the tree. Rocks protruded above the water. The amount of water kept diminishing until there was only a remnant trickle then it also vanished leaving behind a wet riverbed. No stream joined pools rippled by fish. The river had stopped flowing.

The dried up river was greeted by silence. Assembled people stared at each other in disbelief. Silence was soon replaced by a murmur of hostility against the Wild Society. "What have they done now?" an irate voice shouted.

"I knew they'd try something," answered another angry voice.

"They must've made a dam upstream," a voice suggested.

"Maybe beavers," offered another.

"Wild Society beavers," replied a member of a television crew. "We'll get the helicopter and have a look."

Pelican Moon

This statement started excited talking and people dispersed rapidly. People, having access to helicopters, rushed to get them. The Society and Company members obtained helicopters as quickly as possible. They flew northward accompanied by television helicopters speeding above the trail of a wet riverbed containing numerous pools.

Taisse, Sal and Seth were among the last to make the trip. Their helicopter flew above a path of rock, sand, mud and water that had previously been a ribbon of water flowing through the forest. A flowing stream no longer connected pools stirred by fish.

The helicopter proceeded north until glimmering water appeared at Spirit Lake. Most of its water had drained away, exposing the lower border of a rocky shoreline. Helicopters and people were assembled at the site of the old, Mohawk village. Most of the people had gathered at the place where the Fox

River previously flowed from the earth. Now there remained only a still pool of water. The river had stopped emerging from its source.

While a crowd stared at the quiet pool, Casper Forbes asked Seth, "How'd you block the water?"

"I didn't," replied Seth.

"Who did then?" asked Casper.

"You," said Seth.

"Me?" he gasped. "Are you nuts? Why would I want to stop the water? What do you know about this anyway?"

"I know that if you stop trying to develop the Fox River, the water will return," answered Seth.

Casper stared blankly at Seth. Other people milled around quietly. Seth, Taisse and Sal walked back to their helicopter. It returned them to the Society's headquarters.

During the following days, accusations and explanations were exchanged between the Society and the Company. Eventually the Company members faced the fact that without flowing water, the development plans were useless. Company members scrambled to get their money back. Even after this Company had been disbanded, nothing changed with the river.

Sethrum hired a towing company, able to move the largest trucks, to pull the white pine off the riverbed. The tree was placed on the bank. Afterward, Seth, Taisse and other Society members hired an helicopter operator to take them back to the site of the Mohawk village.

They camped near the pool and kept checking its still water. After a few days, during a chorus of bird songs at daybreak, first rays of sunlight flashed over the horizon, shooting wedges of golden light through mist rising from remnant water in Spirit Lake. With light brightening the lake, the pond stirred. Water swirled and gurgled in the pond at the spring before flowing out to become the Fox River. Spirit

Lake refilled while the river flowed as it had earlier. The river had come back to life. Development was not considered again.

EIGHTEEN

OLD TRAILS

Phil and Katherine Dobbs were kept on as managers of Foxwood. Sethrum also restored the resort's connection as a trading post, changing the name to Foxwood Resort and Trading Post.

Sethrum managed the trading post portion of the business. He included old, trade goods together with contemporary merchandise. A specialty was pottery. This work maintained traditional as well as modern methods. All pottery pieces had a trademark, double pelican imprint. The Pelican Pottery House expanded until it included most of the trading post. The pottery house and trading post prospered along with the resort.

The Wild Society members refurbished their headquarters at the hunt camp. These people were also frequent visitors at the log cabin on Sky Mountain.

Much of the past had been maintained in the region. The Mohawk village site continued as before. Spirit Lake changed unnoticeably. The Fox River emerged from the bog at the village site and continued sending a ribbon of water through the wilderness to the restored trading post.

Many people were able to enjoy the preserved beauty of the wilderness. They saw what others had seen previously without having to settle for diluted beauty. The land remained in its original wildness. Visitors saw timelessness in the river valley. They returned to towns with pottery and other trade goods as people had been doing for innumerable years. Modern visitors could still see what those before had seen and kept unaltered in timelessness. The enduring qualities attracted people and restored them with a tonic from the wild.

Cougar was called from his bear rug on the floor of the cabin at Sky Mountain. He left the building with Sethrum to be present during the marriage between Taisse and Sethrum. Cougar was also called into the truck to accompany Taisse and Seth on their honeymoon in the south. Cougar knew most of the places visited such as Will Panther's house in the Smoky Mountains, Sihoki's home next to the river, the Blue Heron Motel and, particularly, the dog races.

Upon returning to the north, Cougar walked the old trails with Seth and Taisse. They enjoyed the pleasures of developed areas and liked to be able to return to wild places such as around the trading post and the long vistas where smoke stood up again from the cabin on Sky Mountain.

Daniel Hance Page

ABOUT THE AUTHOR

Daniel Hance Page is a freelance writer, specialized in environmental and North American Indian issues, with five previous books published and numerous others being written. His books depict the history and culture of the United States and Canada with authentic stories that are spiritual as well as inspirational and are also filled with action, adventure and travel.

Printed in the United States
6297